God Desired
and Desiring

God Desired

Translation by Antonio T. de Nicolás

and Desiring

By JUAN RAMÓN JIMÉNEZ

Introduction by Louis Simpson

PARAGON HOUSE
New York

Second printing

Published in the United States by
Paragon House Publishers
90 Fifth Avenue
New York, New York 10011

Library of Congress Cataloging-in-Publication Data

Jiménez, Juan Ramón, 1881–1958.
  God Desired and Desiring

  Translation of: Dios Deseado y Deseante.
  Bibliography:
  1. God—Poetry. 2. Jiménez, Juan Ramón, 1881–1958—Translations, English. I. Title.
PQ6619.I4A25   1986   861'.62   86-16995
ISBN 0-913729-22-1
ISBN 0-913729-23-X (pbk.)

My soul had already brimmed with sunsets
rolled with the magic currents of the wind
plunged with the tides of the sea
undulated with the perspective of the clouds
cried over green trees on the plains
held the birds and the butterflies on her hand
smiled with the dawn and opened to dreams
in the twilight under closed eyelids, and yet
she never took flight in the light
or in the dark
until she saw an unrequested flame
in the depth of a young eye.

TABLE OF CONTENTS

I. ANIMAL OF DEPTH (1948)

II.   GOD DESIRED AND DESIRING (1949)

III.   ANIMAL OF DEPTH
and
GOD DESIRED AND DESIRING (1948–1952)

UNPUBLISHED POEMS

INTRODUCTION

ANIMAL OF DEPTH (1948). POEMS 1-29.

The god in these poems by Juan Ramón Jiménez is loving-consciousness, made visible through the poet's utterance, "the best I have." The poet listens and is transformed; the world comes alive and enters the poet, "the eternal whole" becoming "the internal all." The poet is changed from being doubtful of the stories about god, into a believer in "the story I have myself created."

Through his desire (listening) for god, the poet discovers that god is desiring: "you love, desiring god, as I love." When the poet was a child he was sad, for he did not understand that the happiness he dreamed of was here; he dreamed of a happiness "beyond sea, beyond earth, beyond sky." He was only half conscious then—and god was only half here, god had not yet entered the poet. As the poet "ran after other things" he lost the essence. But today the world is filled with the consciousness of god.

> I do not know the day it happened, nor under which light
> it came to the garden.

The wearying pursuit of a god under many names—house, sea, mountain— has made way for full consciousness of the one name.

The consciousness of god is fixed in the present, a "country within countries." It appears as a city placed between man and god, a city of harmony that, like a prism, breaks up the light in multiple colors. It is the city of speech, "roses of the mouth," placed between the god desiring the human and the human desiring god. As the opening lines of the first poem stated,

the poet and god are entwined in a "beautiful struggle." The god of loving-consciousness moves towards the poet's "leaps of ecstasy." The image of a mirror describes this moment of the poet's ecstasy—the self and god are perfectly matched. Poems 28 and 29 of *Animal of Depth* continue the rhapsody on this theme, a calm exultation in the possession of full consciousness.

GOD DESIRED AND DESIRING (1949). POEMS 30–36.

The poet, looking back to his childhood, sees that he and god grew together to full consciousness, though the seed of consciousness was always there. Consciousness (the child-god) could not be developed abstractly, through the reasoning mind alone—it had to be developed through nature as feeling:

> ... in a flowering
> of spring,
> in the tiny flower by the hillside,
> the flower made light by pure feeling.

It is through feeling that god is apprehended.

The infinite self and the infinite god (consciousness) meet in the city of expression, that is built on sense-perception: "I stared, smelled and heard, tasted with emotion." The work of expressing god proceeds as a function of the body, "in smelling, in looking, in knowing, in touching/ and in listening to so many entwined lines."

God desiring is the theme of poem 35. We have spoken of the poet's struggle to apprehend god. But god requires the consciousness of the poet: "I am your secret, your diamond." The poet and god are "entwined," the mould and the transparent grace that fills the mold, and are made manifest in the world that "because of you and for you, I have created."

ANIMAL OF DEPTH AND GOD DESIRED AND DESIRING (1948–1952). UNPUBLISHED POEMS. POEMS 37–57.

The thinking that went into *Animal of Depth* and *God Desired and Desiring* was like a storm. It is followed by a calm on which the poet voyages. His consciousness of the god within, desired and desiring, fills him with ecstasy. It is a diamond reddened with his blood ... a dazzling diamond-rose that grows larger until it touches the shore.

But the god that offered himself fully closes up again:

> Now the air, the fire, the water,
> the earth, even love will become barren
> desert, gray and closed to my desire.

Therefore poem 49 affirms the identity of the poet—it was in his life that god found a place for consciousness, in the "passing of the lived life." This is an answer to the vanishing of god—god *cannot* go away.

> Neither in me nor in her
> does one lose the joy of a soft shelter.

But Jiménez says, "I will not be able to go away"—not "god will not be able to go away." The unity of god desired (I) and god desiring (loving-consciousness) has been established. They are indivisibly one, and as it would be impossible for the poet to stand apart from his "lived life," so it is impossible for god to remain withdrawn. The "barren desert, gray and closed" of poem 48 was a moment of doubt injected at the height of affirmation. Such moments do occur . . . "Brightness falls from the air."

The celebration of the created world continues. In "The Naked Infinity" the poet stands on the brink of a temptation: to possess all the kingdoms of the world through imagination. One is reminded of a moment in Scripture, Satan urging Jesus to cast himself from the height and let the angels bear him up. On the brink of "naked infinity" the poet draws back. The poet's eternity is "what I myself am able to conceive of eternity, with all my senses expanded." Imagination is rooted in the senses—it is the eternity of here. The poet invites god to enter his time and space, the "lived life . . . the time I have limited for you in the infinite." The temptation would be to leap into vagueness, "flying in the impossible." But god desires the "lived life"—"I want your name, god, only as origin and end." The poet wants god to become him, a being, a man . . . what the name man means (that is, man with woman). He wants god in the love and bread of every day. The infinity desired is between you, god, and me.

Poem 56 rejects the god people have invented to fill the space between origin and end. The living god is a blank page—to be written on with a pure hand. The poet is listening, and if god does not answer it is not because he is offended. The poet is searching for the truth in beauty. This cannot offend god, nor can it offend beauty.

This is the argument, the struggle of man to attain full consciousness, uttered in these astonishing poems of Juan Ramón Jiménez. He is struggling with his feet planted on the naked earth, as Jacob with the angel. The struggle is in an eternal present, with the body of a living god whose features are the world. The poetry is in the feeling, not in reason, the god people have invented to fill the space between origin and end. The god is made manifest through the lines of the poem, the ecstasy of the word.

To what may this writing be compared? Whitman's "Song of Myself" comes to mind, but it is not with any intention of taking away from Whitman's achievement that I declare a preference for the poetry of Juan Ramón Jiménez—it is both more spiritual and more human—more human because

more spiritual, not cluttered with objects, all the things Whitman felt compelled—Pioneers! O pioneers!—to mention. Jiménez speaks for a higher level of consciousness, a direct and sustained wrestling with consciousness, whereas Whitman speaks of it in hints and flashes.

Religions were originally created on the ground of feelings such as Jiménez utters—including the moment of doubt, of terrifying dismay, when "even love will become barren, desert, gray and closed to my desire." From such depths of the "lived life," the spirit leaps to meet the god that advances toward it.

LOUIS SIMPSON

TRANSLATOR'S NOTES
AND ACKNOWLEDGMENTS

Juan Ramón Jiménez (1881–1958) received the Nobel Prize for Literature in 1956. A very important part of his work, however, did not appear in print till after his death. This is the case with a number of the poems included in this volume. The poems of *Dios Deseado y Deseante* were written at the height of the poet's craft and inspiration. They were all written while the writer lived in the United States. There are fifty–seven poems in all. Thirty–seven were published in Spanish with the title of *"Dios Deseado y Deseante"* and were included in the *Tercera Antología Poética* (1957). There are eighteen additional poems not previously published in Spanish until 1964 by Aguilar, and three other poems that were published in obscure magazines. The whole selection included in this volume was intended to be part of a definitive edition that the poet was *always preparing* but which never came out. The present translation is based on the Spanish edition of 1964 prepared by Antonio Sánchez Barbudo.

The "two" introductions that Juan Ramón Jiménez wrote to the poems are included at the end of this volume. This is how the first one *("Prólogo")* appeared, under the advise of the poet while he was still alive, and the second was written later than most of the poems. All these poems together form what Juan Ramón Jiménez confessed to Ricardo Gullón in 1952: " ... Now this book contains the complete cycle of my thought."[1] It is for this reason that these poems should appear by themselves, as they do in this volume, so that the English reader may become acquainted with one of the most remarkable

---

[1](Conversaciones con Juan Ramón Jiménez. Taurus, Madrid, 1958, p. 119)

experiments in poetry undertaken in the twentieth century by one of its most gifted poets.

This book might appear difficult, if not obscure, even for those readers used to reading poetry. The Introduction to this volume written by another poet, Louis Simpson, should dilute this obscurity to a large extent. The reader, however, should be warned that Juan Ramón Jiménez uses the poetry he makes in this volume to subvert the reader's habits of reading and the expectations of those habits. In this volume, more so than in any other of his writings, Juan Ramón demands as a necessary condition for the reading that the reader focuses primarily on the act itself of creating poetry, "on the god we make when making poetry." The reader must be constantly aware of this orientation, for it is on this condition that the rest of the enchanted world of this volume will open up. The poetic magic will appear only on condition that the reading act and the act of creating poetry agree, and that the poetic descriptions of the external world are momentarily abandoned. It is like trying to break the table in front of us with our bare hand. An expert in karate will focus his concentration on a spot below and away from the surface of the table; the table will break into two as the hand finds its way to the place below. For a non expert the experiment might result in a broken hand. In this, Juan Ramón stands in the company of the best Spanish poetic tradition, including that of Juan de la Cruz (St. John of the Cross).

This translation has been one of both rewards and frustrations. The rewards came from doing what I found to be very close to my own projects in philosophy and poetry, being thus able to feel very much at home in the home of my own tradition. The frustrations came as I tried to translate what I thought I knew so well. In journeying from Spanish into English, my Spanish home followed me, like that of a snail. Fortunately Louis Simpson, a true poet and a true friend, served as midwife, cutting the umbilical cords that kept the translation tied to the original Spanish. The result is the present volume, as close to "an autonomous god," to use Juan Ramón's language, as translations can be. If there is any *accent* left, or there are some other shortcomings, as they are bound to be, they are mine only.

God Desired
and Desiring

I

Animal de Fondo

(1948)

I

Animal of Depth

(1948)

LA TRASPARENCIA, DIOS, LA TRASPARENCIA

Dɪᴏs del venir, te siento entre mis manos,
aquí estás enredado conmigo, en lucha hermosa
de amor, lo mismo
que un fuego con su aire.

No eres mi redentor, ni eres mi ejemplo,
ni mi padre, ni mi hijo, ni mi hermano;
eres igual y uno, eres distinto y todo;
eres dios de lo hermoso conseguido,
conciencia mía de lo hermoso.

Yo nada tengo que purgar.
Toda mi impedimenta
no es sino fundación para este hoy
en que, al fin, te deseo;
porque estás ya a mi lado,
en mi eléctrica zona,
como está en el amor el amor lleno.

Tú, esencia, eres conciencia; mi conciencia
y la de otro, la de todos,
con forma suma de conciencia;
que la esencia es lo sumo,
es la forma suprema conseguible,
y tu esencia está en mí, como mi forma.

Todos mis moldes llenos
estuvieron de ti; pero tú, ahora,
no tienes molde, estás sin molde; eres la gracia
que no admite sostén,
que no admite corona,
que corona y sostiene siendo ingrave.

Eres la gracia libre,
la gloria del gustar, la eterna simpatía,
el gozo del temblor, la luminaria
del clariver, el fondo del amor,
el horizonte que no quita nada;
la trasparencia, dios, la trasparencia,
el uno al fin, dios ahora sólito en lo uno mío,
en el mundo que yo por ti y para ti he creado.

TRANSPARENCY, GOD, TRANSPARENCY

I feel you, god of the future, between my hands,
you are entwined with me, here in a beautiful struggle
of love, just like
fire with its own air.

You are not my redeemer, nor my exemplar,
nor my father, nor my son, nor my brother;
you are the same and one, different and all;
you are the god of the beautiful achieved,
my own consciousness of the beautiful.

I have nothing to atone.
All my excess baggage
is only the foundation that makes today possible,
when, at last, I desire you;
for you already are by my side,
within my electric zone,
as in love all of love is present.

You, essence, are consciousness: my consciousness
and that of others, of all the others,
having the supreme form of consciousness,
for essence is the highest,
the supreme form achievable,
and your essence is in me, as my form.

All my molds have been filled
with you; but you, now,
have no molds, you are formless; you are grace
that has no support,
that accepts no crown,
that crowns and supports being weightless.

You are free grace,
the glory of pleasure, eternal sympathy,
the joy of quivering, the light
of clear sight, the depth of love,
the horizon that sets no boundaries;
transparency, god, transparency,
the one at the end, god now a habit in my unity,
within the world that because of you and for you, I have created.

EL NOMBRE CONSEGUIDO DE LOS NOMBRES

Si yo, por ti, he creado un mundo para ti,
dios, tú tenías seguro que venir a él,
y tú has venido a él, a mi seguro,
porque mi mundo todo era mi esperanza.

Yo he acumulado mi esperanza
en lengua, en nombre hablado, en nombre escrito;
a todo yo le había puesto nombre
y tú has tomado el puesto
de toda esta nombradía.

Ahora puedo yo detener ya mi movimiento,
como la llama se detiene en ascua roja
con resplandor de aire inflamado azul,
en el ascua de mi perpetuo estar y ser;
ahora yo soy ya mi mar paralizado,
el mar que yo decía, mas no duro,
paralizado en olas de conciencia en luz
y vivas hacia arriba todas, hacia arriba.

Todos los nombres que yo puse
al universo que por ti me recreaba yo,
se me están convirtiendo en uno y en un
dios.

El dios que es siempre al fin,
el dios creado y recreado y recreado
por gracia y sin esfuerzo.
El Dios. El nombre conseguido de los nombres.

THE NAME ACHIEVED THROUGH NAMES

If, god, because of you, I have created a world
for you, you definitely had to come to it,
and you have come to it, definitely to me,
because my whole world was my hope.

I have accumulated hope
in language, in spoken names, in written names;
I put a name to everything
and you have taken the place
of all these namings.

Now I can stop my movement,
as the flame stops to become red coal
with the shining air inflamed blue,
within the red-coal of my eternal being and becoming;
now I have at last become my own quiet sea,
the sea I spoke about, but not frozen,
paralyzed into waves of consciousness with light
all alive turning upwards, always upwards.

All the names I gave the universe
which I was recreating for you,
are now turning into one name
and one god.

The god that is always at the end,
god created, recreated and recreated
by grace, with no effort.
God: The name achieved through names.

DE NUESTROS MOVIMIENTOS NATURALES

No solo estás entre los hombres,
dios deseado; estás aquí también en este mar
(desierto más que nunca de hombres)
esperando su paso natural, mi paso,
porque el mar es, tan olvidado,
mundo nuestro de agua.

   Aquí te formas tú con movimiento
permanente de luces y colores,
visible imajen de este movimiento
de tu devenir propio y nuestro devenir.

                                Aquí te formas
hecho inquietud abstracta, fondo
de esa conciencia toda que eres tú.

   Estás aquí en el mar, como formado ya del todo,
como en espera, en plena fe
de nuestros movimientos naturales.

   Aquí estás en ejemplo y en espejo
de la imajinación, de mi imajinación en movimiento,
estás en elemento triple incorporable,
agua, aire, alto fuego,
con la tierra segura en todo el horizonte.

OF OUR NATURAL MOVEMENTS

You are not only among humans,
god desired; you are also here in this sea
(deserted more than ever by humans)
awaiting their natural passage, my passage,
because the sea is, though so forgotten,
our world of water.

Here you take shape with constant movements
of lights and colors,
visible images of this movement
of your own becoming and our own becoming.

Here you take shape
becoming abstract anxiety, depth
of that whole consciousness that you are.

You are here in the sea, as if already fully shaped,
as if waiting, in full faith
for our natural movements.

You are here as exemplar and mirror
of the imagination, of my imagination in movement,
you are in a triple embodiable element,
water, air, high fire,
with the firm earth circling the horizon.

EN MI TERCERO MAR

EN mi tercero mar estabas tú,
de ese color de todos los colores
(que yo dije otro día de tu blanco);
de ese rumor de todos los rumores
que siempre perseguí, con el color,
por aire, tierra, agua, fuego, amor,
tras el gris terminal de todas las salidas.

Tú eras, viniste siendo, eres el amor
en fuego, agua, tierra y aire,
amor en cuerpo mío de hombre y en cuerpo de mujer,
el amor que es la forma
total y única
del elemento natural, que es elemento
del todo, el para siempre;
y que siempre te tuvo y te tendrá,
sino que no todos te ven,
sino que los que te miramos no te vemos hasta un día.

El amor más completo, amor, tú eres,
con la sustancia toda
(y con toda la esencia)
en los sentidos todos de mi cuerpo
(y en todos los sentidos de mi alma)
que son los mismos en el gran saber
de quien, como yo ahora, todo, en luz, lo sabe.

Lo sabe, pues lo supo más y más;
el más, el más, camino único de la sabiduría;
ahora yo sé ya que soy completo,
porque tú, mi deseado dios, estás visible,
estás audible, estás sensible
en rumor y en color de mar, ahora;
porque eres espejo de mí mismo
en el mundo, mayor por ti, que me ha tocado.

IN MY THIRD SEA

You were in my third sea,
of a color made of all colors
(which one day I called your white);
of a sound made of all sounds
which I always chased, as I did color,
through air, earth, water, fire, love,
to the gray terminal of all exits.

You were, you arrived becoming, you are love
in fire, water, earth and air,
love in my male body and in the body of woman,
love that is the total
and unique form
of the natural element, of the element
of the all, of the forever;
and which always had you and will have you,
only all do not see you,
and even those of us looking at you do not see you until one day.

Love, you are the most complete love,
with the whole substance
(and the whole essence)
in each of my bodily senses
(in each of my soul's senses)
which are the same in the great wisdom
of the one, as I am now, who knows all in the light.

He knows it, for he knew it more and more;
that more, that more is the only road to wisdom;
now I know that I am complete,
for you, my desired god, are visible,
audible, touchable
within the sound and the color of the sea, right now;
for you are the mirror of myself
in the world, made larger because of you, that I live in.

TODAS LAS NUBES ARDEN

TODAS las nubes arden
porque yo te he encontrado,
dios deseante y deseado;
antorchas altas cárdenas
(granas, azules, rojas, amarillas)
en alto grito de rumor de luz.

Del redondo horizonte vienen todas
en congregación fúljida,
a abrazarse con vueltas de esperanza
a mi fe respondida.

(Mar desierto, con dios
en redonda conciencia
que me habla y me canta,
que me confía y me asegura;
por ti yo paso en pie
alerta, en mí afirmado,
conforme con que mi viaje
es al hombre seguido, que me espera
en puerto de llegada permanente,
de encuentro repetido).

Todas las nubes que existieron,
que existen y que existirán,
me rodean con signos de evidencia;
ellas son para mí
la afirmación alzada de este hondo
fondo de aire en que yo vivo;
el subir verdadero del subir,
el subir del hallazgo en lo alto profundo.

ALL THE CLOUDS ARE BURNING

All the clouds are burning
because I found you,
god desiring and desired;
tall purple torches
(scarlet, blue, red, yellow)
in a high scream of the sound of light.

They all come from the round horizon
in shining congregation,
to embrace each other with a return of hope
to my answered faith.

(Abandoned sea with god
in rounded consciousness
speaking and singing to me,
who trusts me and reassures me;
I pass over you with a vigilant
foot placed on myself,
agreeing that my journey
follows the man pursued, who waits for me
at a permanent port of arrival,
of repeated encounters.)

All the clouds that were,
that are, that will be,
surround me with signs;
they are to me
the high affirmation of this deep
depth of air within which I live;
the true climb of climbing,
the climb of the discovery made in the highest depth.

LA FRUTA DE MI FLOR

Esta conciencia que me rodeó
en toda mi vivida,
como halo, aura, atmósfera de mi ser mío,
se me ha metido ahora dentro.

Ahora el halo es de dentro
y ahora es mi cuerpo centro
visible de mí mismo; soy, visible,
cuerpo maduro de este halo,
lo mismo que la fruta, que fue flor
de ella misma, es ahora la fruta de mi flor.

La fruta de mi flor soy, hoy, por ti,
dios deseado y deseante,
siempre verde, florido, fruteado,
y dorado y nevado, y verdecido
otra vez (estación total toda en un punto)
sin más tiempo ni espacio
que el de mi pecho, esta
mi cabeza sentida palpitante,
toda cuerpo, alma míos
(con la semilla siempre
del más antiguo corazón).

Dios, ya soy la envoltura de mi centro,
de ti dentro.

THE FRUIT OF MY FLOWER

This consciousness that surrounded me
in all of my lived life,
like a halo, aura, the air of my own being,
has now entered within me.

Now the halo is from within
and my body is now the visible
center of myself; I am visible,
the grown body of this halo,
as a fruit, which was a flower
of itself, is now the fruit of my flower.

Today I am the fruit of my flower, because of you,
god desired and desiring,
always green, blooming, heavy with fruit,
also golden, snowy, and again
made green (a whole season in one instant)
with no other time nor space
than that of my chest, this,
my head feeling it throb,
all turned into body, all my soul
(always with the seed
of the most ancient heart).

God, I am the wrapping of my center,
of you within.

CONCIENCIA PLENA

Tú me llevas, conciencia plena, deseante dios,
por todo el mundo.
                    En este mar tercero,
casi oigo tu voz; tu voz del viento
ocupante total del movimiento;
de los colores, de las luces
eternos y marinos.

   Tu voz de fuego blanco
en la totalidad del agua, el barco, el cielo,
lineando las rutas con delicia,
grabándome con fúljido mi órbita segura
de cuerpo negro
con el diamante lúcido en su dentro.

FULL CONSCIOUSNESS

You take me, full consciousness, god desiring,
through the whole world.
Within this third sea,
I almost hear your voice; your voice, the wind,
inhabitant of total movement;
of colors, of lights
eternal and marine.

Your voice of white fire
within the totality of water, ship, sky,
tracing the routes with delicacy,
tracing with light my certain orbit
of a black body
housing the bright diamond inside.

AL CENTRO RAYEANTE

TÚ estás entre los cúmulos
oro del cielo azul,
los cúmulos radiantes
del redondo horizonte desertado
por el hombre embaucado,
dios deseante y deseado;
estas formas que llegan al cenit
sobre el timón, adelantadas, y acompasan
el movimiento escelso, lento,
insigne cabeceo de una proa,
cruzándose con su subir, con su bajar
contra el sur, contra el sur,
enhiesta, enhiesta como un pecho jadeante.

Tú vienes con mi norte hacia mi sur,
tú vienes de mi este hacia mi oeste,
tú me acompañas, cruce único, y me guías
entre los cuatro puntos inmortales,
dejándome en su centro siempre y en mi centro
que es tu centro.

Todo está dirijido
a este tesoro palpitante,
dios deseado y deseante,
de mi mina en que espera mi diamante;
a este rayeado movimiento
de entraña abierta (en su alma) con el sol
del día, que te va pasando en éstasis,
a la noche, en el trueque más gustoso
conocido, de amor y de infinito.

TOWARDS THE RADIANT CENTER

You are among the gold
cumulus of the blue sky,
the radiant cumulus
of the round horizon deserted
by the deceived man,
god desiring and desired;
these shapes that reach the zenith
riding the helm, ahead, and keeping time
to the slow, solemn movement,
deliberate nodding of the prow,
crossing its ups and then its downs
against the south, against the south,
upright, upright like a heaving breast.

You come from my north towards my south,
you come from my east towards my west,
you accompany me, unique crossing, and guide me
across the four immortal points,
leaving me always at their center, my center,
which is your center.

All aims
at this throbbing treasure,
god desired and desiring,
of the mine where my diamond waits;
at this radiant movement
of an open womb (within its soul) with the sun
of day, which carries you in ecstasy,
into the night, in the most pleasurable exchange
known, of love and infinity.

LO MAJICO ESENCIAL NOMBRADO

EN esa isla que la luna,
tras una nube negra, echa al mar lejano,
estás tú, como espejo caído luna arriba,
por amor a este mar y a quien lo pasa
y por amor al ámbito completo.

Esa congregación, ojos de plata
fundida en pensamiento miriante
tuyo, dios deseado y deseante,
es el oasis definido
de mi limpio ideal unánime.

Que es él, y tu reflejo
de ti en conciencia, de ti exacto:
paz, claridad, delicia iguales a sus nombres,
conciencia diosa una,
disfrutadora y disfrutada mía,
disfrute de lo májico esencial nombrado.

THE MAGIC ESSENTIALLY NAMED

You are
upon an island, that the moon
from behind a black cloud has thrown into the distant sea,
like a fallen mirror with its face up,
in love with this sea and whoever crosses it,
in love with the whole horizon.

That congregation, eyes of silver
melted into reflecting thought
of you, god desired and desiring,
is the defined oasis
of my unanimous, taintless ideal.

For this, and the reflection
of you in consciousness, is just like you;
peace, clarity, joy equal to the names,
only one divine consciousness
enjoying and enjoyed by me,
enjoyment of the magic essentially named.

CONCIENCIA HOY AZUL

(Dios está azul . . .
ANTES)

CONCIENCIA de hondo azul del día, hoy
concentración de trasparencia azul;
mar que sube a mi mano a darme sed
de mar y cielo en mar,
en olas abrazantes, de sal viva.

Mañana de verdad en fondo de aire
(cielo del agua fondo
de otro vivir aún en inmanencia)
esplosión suficiente (nobe, ola, espuma
de ola y nube)
para llevarme en cuerpo y alma
al ámbito de todos los confines,
a ser el yo que anhelo
y a ser el tú que anhelas en mi anhelo,
conciencia hoy de vasto azul,
conciencia deseante y deseada,
dios hoy azul, azul, azul y más azul,
igual que el dios de mi Moguer azul,
un día.

CONSCIOUSNESS TODAY BLUE

"God is blue ... "

Consciousness of deep blue of the day, today
concentration of blue transparency;
sea that climbs to my hand to make me thirsty
for the sea and the sky on the sea,
in embracing waves of living salt.

Morning of truth against a depth of air
(sky of the water, depth
of a different life still in immanence)
sufficient explosion (cloud, wave, foam
of wave and cloud)
to carry me in body and soul
to the threshold of all boundaries,
to become the I I long for
and to become the you you long for in my longing,
consciousness of vast blue today,
consciousness desiring and desired,
god today blue, blue, blue and more blue,
just like the god of my blue Moguer,
once.

SIN TEDIO NI DESCANSO

Si yo he salido tanto al mundo,
ha sido solo y siempre
para encontrarte, deseado dios,
entre tanta cabeza y tanto pecho
de tanto hombre.

(Ciudad jigante, gran concurso,
que a mí vuelves en espejismo gris de agua,
en este sol azul del sur de luz,
de este dios deseante y deseado,
ojos y ojos y ojos
con destellos movientes instantáneos
de lo eterno en camino.)

¡Tanto motor de pensamiento y sentimiento
(negro, blanco, amarillo, rojo, verde
de cuerpo) con el alma
derivando hacia ti,
deviniendo hacia sí,
sucediendo hacia mí,
sin saberlo o sabiéndolo yo y ellos!

Designio universal, en llamas
de sombras y de luces inquirientes
y esperantes,
de ojo acechador inmenso que te espía
con pena o alegría
de trajinante andanza aventurera.

Y yo poseedor, enmedio, ya,
de tu conciencia, dios, por esperarte
desde mi infancia destinada,
sin descanso ni tedio.

WITHOUT BOREDOM OR REST

If I have gone so much out into the world
it has only and always been
in order to find you, god desired,
among so many heads and breasts
of so many men.

(Giant city, large gathering,
coming back to me in a gray mirage of water,
in the blue sun of the south of light,
of this god desiring and desired,
eyes and eyes and eyes
with sudden flashes
of the eternal on the way.)

So many engines of thought and feeling
(black, white, yellow, red, green
of body) with their souls
drifting towards you,
moving towards themselves,
acting for me,
not knowing, or knowing, they and I!

Universal design in flames
of expectant and questioning shadows
and lights,
of an immense and watchful eye spying on one
with the pain or gladness
of an adventurous and busy happening.

And I the owner, in the middle, now
of your consciousness, god, because I have waited for you
since my fated infancy,
without rest or boredom.

DESPIERTO A MEDIODIA

EL mar siempre despierto,
el mar despierto ahora también a mediodía,
cuando todos reposan menos yo y tú
(o el que trabaja con la hora fija, fuera)
me da mejor que nadie y nada tu conciencia,
dios deseante y deseado,
que surjes, desvelado
vijilante del ocio suficiente,
de la sombra y la luz, en pleamar fundida,
fundido en pleamar.

Tus rayos reespedidos de ti son
mensajes hacia el sol,
fuentes de luminoso y blanco oro surtidor
que refrescan la vida al todo blanco sol.

Y el pleno sol te llena, con su carbón dentro,
como la luna anoche te llenaba,
y cual eras la luna, el sol eres tú solo,
solo, pues que eres todo.

Conciencia en pleamar y pleacielo,
en pleadiós, en éstasis obrante universal.

AWAKE AT MIDDAY

The sea awake always,
the sea awake now too at midday,
when all are resting except you and me
(or whoever works by a fixed time, outside)
your consciousness suits me better than any one or any thing,
god desiring and desired,
who springs awake
watching the sufficient leisure,
of the shadow and the light, melting on the high tide,
melted on the surface of the sea.

Your rays reissued from you are
messages towards the sun,
fountains of luminous and white spouting gold
that refresh all life against an all white sun.

And the full sun fills you, with its coal from within,
as the moon filled you last night,
and as you were the moon, you alone are the sun,
you alone, for you are all.

Consciousness of high tide, of high sky,
of high god, in ecstasy, the universal maker.

LA FORMA QUE ME QUEDA

ENTRE la arboladura serena y la alta nube
que mi cristal limita en círculo completo,
tú te asomas, dios deseante, sonriendo
con el levante matinero, a verme despertar;
y me despierto sonriendo yo también
a este sueño en vijilia que me invita.

Y entre todos mis sueños, dios, en momentáneos
alertas, bienestar de lo dormido,
tú intercalabas, deseado,
como las olas oro de este mar,
esta seguridad que ahora me ocupa
mi día con mi noche, mi noche con mi día.

Y ahora, cambiando el sueño en acto,
¡qué dinamismo me levanta
y me obliga a creer que esto que hago
es lo que puedo, debo, quiero hacer;
este trabajo tan gustoso de contarte,
de contarme de todas las maneras, en la forma
que me quedó de todas, para ti!

THE FORM I AM LEFT

Between the calm forest of masts and the high cloud
that my porthole glass frames in a full circle,
you peer in, god desiring, smiling
with the sunrise, to see me awaken;
and I awaken smiling too
to that sleep in vigil inviting me.

And between my dreams, god, in momentary
flashes, well being of sleep,
you interjected, god desired,
as the gold waves of this sea,
this certainty that now links
my day with my night, my night with my day.

And now with the dream turned reality,
what energy uplifts me
and forces me to believe that what I do
is what I can, must, wish to do;
this task with such pleasure in telling you,
in telling you in every way, in the only way
that of all others was left to me, for you!

QUE SE VE SER

En la mañana oscura,
una luz que no sé de dónde viene,
que no se ve venir, que se ve ser
fuente total, invade lo completo.

Un ser de luz, que es todo y solo luz,
luz vividora y luz vivificante;
una conciencia diamantina en dios,
un dios en ascua blanca,
que sustenta, que incita y que decide
en la mañana oscura.

SEEING IT BE

On the dark morning,
a light that comes from I know not where,
that is not seen coming, is seen to be
the total fountain, invading what is complete.

A being of light, all and only light,
living light and life-giving light;
a diamond-colored consciousness in god,
a god turned into a white burning coal,
sustaining, inciting and deciding
in the dark morning.

CON LA CRUZ DEL SUR

LA cruz del sur se echa en una nube
y me mira con ojos diamantinos
mis ojos más profundos que el amor,
con un amor de siempre conocida.

Estuvo, estuvo, estuvo
en todo el cielo azul de mi inmanencia;
eran sus cuatro ojos la conciencia
limpia, la sucesiva solución de una hermosura
que me esperaba en la cometa,
ya, que yo remontaba cuando niño.

Y yo he llegado, ya he llegado,
en mi penúltima jornada de ilusión
del dios consciente de mí y mío,
a besarle los ojos, sus estrellas,
con cuatro besos solos de amor vivo;
el primero, en los ojos de su frente;
el segundo, el tercero, en los ojos de sus manos,
y el cuarto, en ese ojo de su pie de alta sirena.

La cruz del sur me está velando
en mi inocencia última,
en mi volver al niñodiós que yo fui un día
en mi Moguer de España.

Y abajo, muy debajo de mí, en tierra subidísima,
que llega a mi exactísimo ahondar,
una madre callada de boca me sustenta,
como me sustentó en su falda viva,
cuando yo remontaba mis cometas blancas;
y siente ya conmigo todas las estrellas
de la redonda, plena eternidad nocturna.

WITH THE SOUTHERN CROSS

The Southern Cross lies down on a cloud
and looks at me with diamond-bright eyes
into my eyes deeper than love,
with a love of the forever known.

It was, it was, it was
in the whole blue sky of my immanence;
its four eyes were the clear
conscience, the successive solutions of a beauty
waiting for me already in the kite
that I, as a child, used to fly.

And I have arrived, at last arrived
in this my penultimate joyful discovery
of the god conscious of me and mine,
to kiss his eyes, his stars,
with only four kisses of living love;
the first on the eyes of his forehead;
the second, third, on the eyes of his hands
and the fourth, on the eye on the mermaid's sailing foot.

The Southern Cross is watching over me
in my last innocence,
on my return to the child-god I was, once
in my Moguer of Spain.

And below, far below me, upon a very high earth,
that reaches my most exact remembering,
a mother with mute voice nourishes me,
as she used to nourish me upon her living lap,
when I used to fly my white kites;
and now she feels with me all the stars
of the round, full, nocturnal eternity.

EN IGUALDAD SEGURA DE ESPRESION

¿EL perro está ladrando a mi conciencia,
a mi dios en conciencia,
como a una luna de inminencia hermosa?

¿La ve lucir, en esta inmensa noche,
por la sombra estrellada de todas las estrellas
acojedoras de su cruz del sur,
que son como mi palio
descendido por ansia y por amor?

(Este palio que siento que eterniza
mi luz, mi misteriosa luz, mi luz,
una hermana contenta de su luz.)

El perro viene, y lo acaricio;
me acaricia, y me mira como un hombre,
con la hermandad completa
de la noche serena y señalada.

El siente (yo lo siento) que le hago
la caricia que espera un perro desde siempre,
la caricia tranquila del callado
en igualdad segura de espresión.

IN EQUAL ASSURANCE OF EXPRESSION

Is the dog barking at my consciousness,
at my god in consciousness,
as at a moon imminently beautiful?

Does he see it shine, in this immense night,
through the starry shadows of all the stars
sheltering the Southern Cross,
which to me are like my canopy
lowered, through desire and love?

(This canopy I feel makes my light
eternal, my mysterious light, my light,
a happy sister of her light.)

The dog comes to me and I pet him;
he caresses me, and looks at me like a man,
with the full fraternity
of the sparkling and serene night.

He feels (I feel it) that I give him
the petting a dog always waits for,
the tranquil petting of silence
in equal assurance of expression.

ESA ORBITA ABIERTA

Los pájaros del aire
se mecen en las ramas de las nubes,
los pájaros del agua
se mecen en las nubes de la mar
(y viento, lluvia, espuma, sol en torno)
como yo, dios, me mezco en los embates
de ola y rama, viento y sol, espuma y lluvia
de tu conciencia mecedora bienandante.

    (¿No es el goce
mayor de lo divino de lo humano
el dejarse mecer en dios, en la conciencia
regazada de Dios, en la inmanencia madreada,
con su vaivén seguro interminable?)

    Va y ven, el movimiento
de lo eterno que vuelve, en ello mismo
y en uno mismo;
esa órbita abierta
que no se sale de sí nunca, abierta,
y que nunca se libra de sí, abierta
(porque)
lo cerrado no existe en su infinito
aunque sea regazo y madre y gloria.

THAT OPEN ORBIT

The birds of the air
rock in the branches of the clouds,
the birds of the water
rock in the clouds of the sea
(with wind, rain, foam, sun all around)
just as I, god, rock myself in the swings
of wave and branch, wind and sun, foam and rain
of your consciousness, rocking also while it moves.

(Is it not the greatest
joy of the divine, of the human
to let oneself be rocked in god, in the womb-like
consciousness of god, in the mothering immanence,
with its secure, interminable sway?)

Come and go, to and fro, the movement
of the eternal returning, in its own movement
and in one self;
the open orbit
that never goes beyond itself, open,
that is never free of itself, open,
(because)
what is closed does not exist in its infinity
even though it be womb and mother and glory.

EN AMOROSO LLENAR

TODOS vamos, tranquilos, trabajando:
el maquinista, fogueando; el vijilante,
datando; el timonel, guiando;
el pintor, pintando; el radiotelegrafista,
escuchando; el carpintero, martilleando;
el capitán, dictando; la mujer,
cuidando, suspirando, palpitando.

. . . Y yo, dios deseante, deseando;
yo que te estoy llenando, en amoroso
llenar, en última conciencia mía,
como el sol o la luna, dios,
de un mundo todo uno para todos.

IN LOVING PENETRATION

We all move about, calmly, working;
the engineer making steam; the watchman
taking data; the helmsman steering;
the painter painting; the wireless operator
listening; the carpenter hammering;
the captain giving orders; women
caring, sighing, palpitating.

. . . And I, god desired, desiring;
I who am filling you in loving
penetration in my deepest consciousness,
like the sun or the moon, god,
from a world made one for everyone.

PARA QUE YO TE OIGA

RUMOR del mar que no te oyes
tú mismo, mar, pero que te oigo yo
con este oír a que he llegado
en mi dios deseante y deseado
y que, con él, escucho como él.

Con oído de dios te escucho, mar,
verdemar y amarillomar saltado,
donde el albatros y la gaviota
nos ven pasar, amando en su lugar
(su ola que se cambia y que se queda)
oyéndote a ti, mar, ellos también,
pero sin saber nada de que yo
sé que tú no te oyes.

Para que yo te oiga, mi conciencia
en dios me abre tu ser todo para mí,
y tú me entras en tu gran rumor,
la infinita rapsodia de tu amor
que yo sé que es de amor, pues que es tan bella.

¡Que es tan bella, aunque tú,
mar amarillo y verde, no lo sepas acaso todavía,
pero que yo lo sé escuchándola; y la cuento
(para que no se pierda) en la canción
sucesiva del mundo en que va el hombre
llevándote, con él, a su dios solo!

SO THAT I MAY HEAR YOU

Sound of the sea not able to hear yourself,
sea, but I am able to hear you
with the listening I have achieved
in my god desiring and desired
and that, with him, I hear as he does.

I listen to you with the ear of god, sea,
green-sea and choppy, yellow-sea,
where the albatross and the seagull
watch us pass, making love in their places
(their wave that changes and stays)
listening to you, sea, in their own way,
for they do not know that I know
you cannot hear yourself.

So that I may hear you, my consciousness
in god opens your being wide to me,
and you enter me with your murmur
that I know is of love, for it is so beautiful.

It is so beautiful, even though you,
yellow and green sea, might not yet know it,
but I know in listening to it; and I tell it
(so that it will not be lost) in a continual song
of the world where men walk about carrying you
with them to their lonely god!

EN LO MEJOR QUE TENGO

MAR verde y cielo gris y cielo azul
y albatros amorosos en la ola,
y en todo, el sol, y tú en el sol, mirante
dios deseado y deseante,
alumbrando de oros distintos mi llegada;
la llegada de este que soy ahora yo,
de este que ayer mismo yo dudaba
de que pudiera ser en ti como lo soy.

¡Qué trueque de hombre en mí, dios deseante,
de ser dudón en la leyenda
del dios de tantos decidores,
a ser creyente firme
en la historia que yo mismo he creado
desde toda mi vida para ti!

Ahora llego yo a este término
de un año de mi vida natural,
en mi fondo de aire en que te tengo,
encima de este mar, fondo de agua;
este término hermoso cegador
al que me vas entrando tú,
contento de ser tuyo y de ser mío
en lo mejor que tengo, mi espresión.

THE BEST I HAVE

Green sea, gray sky, blue sky,
albatrosses in amorous play on the waves
and over everything the sun, and you in the sun, witnessing,
god desired and desiring,
lighting my arrival with different golds;
the arrival of this one I am now,
this one that yesterday I doubted
I could be inside you, even though I am.

What a transformation of the man in me, god desiring,
from being doubtful of the stories
about god of so many preachers,
to become a firm believer
in the story I have myself created
from the beginning of my life for you!

Now I have come to the end
of this one year of my natural life,
upon the depth of air on which I have you,
riding this sea over a depth of water;
this beautiful, blinding end
to which you yourself are leading me,
happy to belong to you and to myself
in the best I have, my expression.

EL TODO INTERNO

He llegado a una tierra de llegada.
Me esperaban los tuyos, deseado dios;
me esperaban los míos
que, en mi anhelar de tantos años tuyos,
me esperaron contigo,
conmigo te esperaron.

¡Y qué luz entre ellos:
en un sol cenital imprevisto y sonllorante,
sobre una aurora con sus torres contra rojo,
en una noche de encantado desear,
en una tarde de crepúsculo alargado,
entre un mediodía de plomo abrigador,
por una madrugada con nublado y una estrella!

¡Qué luz entre ojos, labios, manos;
qué primavera del latir;
qué tú entre ellos, en nosotros tú;
qué luz, qué perspectivas
de pecho y frente (joven, mayor, niño);
qué cantar, qué decir,
qué abrazar, qué besar;
qué elevación de ti en nosotros
hasta llegar a ti,
a este tú que te pones sobre ti
para que todos lleguen por la escala
de carne y alma
a la conciencia desvelada que es el astro
que acumula y completa, en unificación,
todos los astros en el todo eterno!

El todo eterno que es el todo interno.

THE INTERNAL ALL

I have arrived at a place of arrival.
Your own people were waiting for me, god desired;
my own people were waiting for me,
who, after waiting for you for so many of your years,
waited for me with you,
waited for you with me.

And how much light came from them:
from a high sun, sudden and loud,
against a dawn with reddening towers,
on a night of enchanted desires,
on an evening of prolonged twilight,
from a midday of sheltering lead,
from an early morning with clouds and one star!

How much light from eyes, lips, hands;
what a springtime of palpitations;
how you were among them, you in us;
how much light, what perspectives
of chest and forehead (young, old, child);
what songs, what speeches,
what embraces, what kisses;
what an uplifting of you in us
to make us reach you,
this you you cover yourself with
so that all may ascend by the stairs
of flesh and soul
to the awakened consciousness that is the star
that accumulates and completes, in unification,
all the stars in the eternal whole!

The eternal whole is the internal all.

RIO-MAR-DESIERTO

A ti he llegado, riomar,
desiertoriomar de onda y de duna,
de simún y tornado, también, dios;
mar para el pie y para el brazo,
con el ala en el brazo y en el pie.

Nunca me lo dijeron.
Y llego a ti por mí en mi hora, y te descubro;
te descubro con dios, dios deseante,
que me dice que eras siempre suyo,
que eras siempre también mío
y te me ofreces en sus ojos
como una gran visión que me faltaba.

Tú me das movimiento en solidez,
movimiento más lento, pues que voy
hacia mi movimiento detenido;
movimiento de plácida conciencia
de amor con más arena,
arena que llevar bajo la muerte
(la corriente infinita que ya dije)
como algo incorruptible.

Por ti,
desierto mar del río de mi vida,
hago tierra mi mar,
me gozo en ese mar (que yo decía
que no era de mi tierra);
por ti mi fondo de animal de aire se hace
más igual; y la imajen
de mi devenir fiel a la belleza
se va igualando más hacia mi fin,
fundiendo el dinamismo con el éstasis.

Mar para poder yo con mis dos manos
palpar, cojer, fundir el ritmo de mi ser escrito,
igualarlo en la ola de agua y tierra.

DESERT-SEA-RIVER

I have come to you, seariver,
desertriversea of wave and dune,
of simoon and tornado too, god;
sea for the foot and the arm,
with a wing on the arm and on the foot.

They never told me.
But I come to you by myself in my own hour to discover you;
I discover you with god, god desiring,
who tells me you are always his,
that you are also mine always,
and you offer yourself to me in his eyes
as the grand vision I was lacking.

You give me movement on solid ground,
a slower movement, for I am moving
toward my arrested movement;
movement of placid consciousness
of love mixed with sand,
sand to smuggle past death
(the infinite current I have already mentioned)
as something incorruptible.

Because of you,
seadesert of the river of my life,
I turn my sea into land,
I rejoice in that sea (I used to say
it did not belong to my land);
because of you my depth of animal of air
exists; and the image
of my becoming faithful to beauty
is becoming more real towards the end,
where movement and ecstasy melt.

This sea makes it possible for my two hands
to touch, grab, melt the rhythm of my written being,
and make it even with the wave of water and earth.

RIO-MAR-DESIERTO (*continuación*)

Por mí, mi riomardesierto,
la imajen de mi obra en dios final
no es ya la ola detenida,
sino la tierra solo detenida
que fue inquieta, inquieta, inquieta.

DESERT-SEA-RIVER (*continued*)

Because of me, desertseariver,
the image of my work in the final god
is no longer the arrested wave,
but the earth only momentarily held still
where it used to be restless, restless, restless.

EN LA CIRCUMBRE

Tú estás, dios deseado, en la circumbre,
dominándolo todo,
lo redondo y lo alto,
desde una nube negra abierta en chispas.

Todos te ven; todos te vemos;
desde las azoteas con los límites
abiertos; desde los balcones
y su jaula de impulso bajo, inquieto pie;
desde los cuartos de la intelijencia
sensitiva; desde los corredores;
desde los cepos del instante bruto;
desde los sótanos del relegado fiel.

A todos llegas tú por tus mil lados;
en todos vives tú con tus mil ecos;
no hay chispa tuya que no hiera
un ojo alegre o triste.

Tú eres corona en pie que todos pueden
quitarse de la cálida cabeza
y dejarla en el beso recaída.

Porque tú amas, deseante dios, como yo amo.

IN THE CIRCUMPEAK

You are, god desired, in the circumpeak,
overseeing everything,
what is round and what is high,
from a dark cloud throwing out sparks.

Everyone sees you; all of us see you;
from the roof top with open
boundaries; from the balconies
with their bird cage of short leaps, uncertain footing;
from the rooms of the sensitive
intelligence; from the corridors;
from the traps of the naked instant;
from the cellars of the faithful who have been abandoned.

You arrive to each one from your thousand sides;
in each you live with your thousand echoes;
there is no spark from you that does not wound
a human eye, happy or sad.

You are a standing crown that each
may remove from the warm head
and leave fallen again with a kiss.

Because you love, desiring god, as I love.

CON MI MITAD ALLI

¡Mi plata aquí en el sur, en este sur,
conciencia en plata lucidera, palpitando
en la mañana limpia,
cuando la primavera saca flor a mis entrañas!

Mi plata, aquí, respuesta de la plata
que soñaba esta plata en la mañana limpia
de mi Moguer de plata,
de mi Puerto de plata,
de mi Cádiz de plata,
niño yo triste soñeando siempre
el ultramar, con la ultratierra, el ultracielo.

Y el ultracielo estaba aquí
con esta tierra, la ultratierra,
este ultramar, con este mar;
y aquí, en este ultramar, mi hombre encontró,
norte y sur, su conciencia plenitente,
porque esta le faltaba.

Y estoy alegre de alegría llena,
con mi mitad allí, mi allí, complementándome,
pues que ya tengo mi totalidad,
la plata mía aquí en el sur, en este sur.

WITH MY HALF THERE

My silver here in the south, in this south,
consciousness in shining silver, palpitating
in the clear morning,
when spring brings out flowers from my flesh!

My silver, here, an answer to the dreamed
silver of this silver of the clear morning
of my Moguer of silver,
of my Puerto of silver,
of my Cádiz of silver,
a sad child I, always dreaming
of beyond sea, beyond earth, beyond sky.

But the sky beyond was here
with this earth, this beyond earth,
this beyond sea, in this sea;
and here, in this sea beyond, my manhood found,
north and south, its fulfilling consciousness,
for this it was lacking.

Now I am happy with full happiness,
with my half there, my there, my full complement,
for now I have my totality,
my own silver here in the south, in this south.

TAL COMO ESTABAS

En el recuerdo estás tal como estabas.
Mi conciencia ya era esta conciencia,
pero yo estaba triste, siempre triste,
porque aún mi presencia no era la semejante
de esta final conciencia.

Entre aquellos jeranios, bajo aquel limón,
junto a aquel pozo, con aquella niña,
tu luz estaba allí, dios deseante;
tú estabas a mi lado,
dios deseado,
pero no habías entrado todavía en mí.

El sol, el azul, el oro eran,
como la luna y las estrellas,
tu chispear y tu coloración completa,
pero yo no podía cojerte con tu esencia,
la esencia se me iba
(como la mariposa de la forma)
porque la forma estaba en mí
y al correr tras lo otro la dejaba;
tanto, tan fiel que la llevaba,
que no me parecía lo que era.

Y hoy, así, sin yo saber por qué,
la tengo entera, entera.
No sé qué día fue ni con qué luz
vino a un jardín, tal vez, casa, mar, monte,
y vi que era mi nombre sin mi nombre,
sin mi sombra, mi nombre,
el nombre que yo tuve antes de ser
oculto en este ser que me cansaba,
porque no era este ser que hoy he fijado
(que pude no fijar)
para todo el futuro iluminado
iluminante,
dios deseado y deseante.

JUST AS YOU WERE

In memory you are just as you were.
My consciousness was already this consciousness,
but I was sad, always sad,
because my presence was not yet the equal
of this final consciousness.

Among those geraniums, under that lemon tree,
next to that well, with that girl,
your light was there, god desiring;
you were by my side,
god desired,
but you had not yet entered me.

The sun, the blue, the gold were
as the moon and the stars,
your sparks and complete spectrum,
but I was unable to grasp you in your essence,
your essence would flee me
(as a butterfly from its shape)
for the shape was in me
and as I ran after other things I would lose it;
so much, so faithfully I carried it
that it did not seem what it was.

But today, just like that, not knowing why,
I have it whole, whole.
I do not know the day it happened, nor under which light
it came to the garden, maybe house, sea, mountain,
and I saw it was my name without my name,
the name I had before I became
hidden in this being that tired me,
because it was not this being I have framed
(which I could not frame)
for the rest of the illuminated future
illuminating,
god desired and desiring.

EN PAIS DE PAISES

En estas perspectivas ciudadales
que la vida suceden, como prismas,
con su sangre de tiempo en el cojido espacio,
tú, conciencia de dios, eres presente fijo,
esencia tesorera de dios mío,
con todas las edades
de colores, de músicas, de voces,
en país de países.

Y en ellas, simultánea
creencia de fijados paraísos de fondo,
te sucedes también, conciencia y dios
intercalado de verdores nuevos,
de niñas de color solar,
de cobre retenido en adiós largo,
que componen tu sólita estación total,
tu intemporalidad tan realizada en mí.

Armoniosa suprema, ciudad rica
de arquitecturas graduadas que descifro yo
desde arriba, con ojos reposantes;
música de la cúbica visión de blancos sucedidos
donde coloca el cuerpialma
su contrastado oasis del volver,
del volver, del volver y del volver,
con vida melodiosa en cada corte.
¡Las arpas de la óptica alegría,
dios; los concientes planos de las glorias
posibles a este pie de amor establecido!

¡Qué abrirse de la boca de las rosas,
las rosas de la boca, en estas hojas
practicables al ojo enamorado
que encuentra su descanso repetible
de los dos infinitos; tan posible
existir, existir mío
en suficiente estar aquí la vida entera!

Un corazón de rosa construida
entre tú, dios deseante de mi vida,
y, deseante de tu vida, yo.

A COUNTRY WITHIN COUNTRIES

Within these citified perspectives
cutting up life in succession, like prisms,
their blood of time within the stolen spaces,
you consciousness of god, become the fixed present,
treasuring the essence of my god,
holding all the ages
of colors, music, voices
in a country within countries.

And in them, a simultaneous
faith made of still paradises of depth,
you also appear in discontinuity, consciousness and god
imprinted with new floral greens,
with girls colored by the sun,
with copper lingering in prolonged goodbyes,
which form your customary total season,
your intemporality so imprinted in me.

Supreme harmony, rich city
in graded architecture which I decipher
from above, with tranquil eyes;
music of a cubic vision of white colors
following each other where the bodysoul
places its contrasting oasis of the return,
of the return, of the return and of the return,
with melodious life in every edge.
Harps of the optic joy,
god; conscious planes of the possible
glories upon this foundation of love!

How the mouth of roses opens,
the roses of the mouth, in these
manageable pages to the eye in love
which finds repeatable rest
in the two infinites; such a possible
existence, my existence
sufficiently set here for life eternal!

A heart of rose built
between you, god desiring my life,
and me, desiring yours.

POR TANTO PEREGRINO

Dios en conciencia, caes sobre el mundo,
como un beso completo de una cara entera,
en plano contentar de todos los deseos.
La luz del mediodía
no es sino tu absoluto resplandor;
y hasta los más oscuros escondrijos
la penetran contigo,
con alegría de alta posesión de vida.

El estar tuyo contra mí
es tu secuencia natural; y eres
espejo mío abierto en un inmenso abrazo
(el espejo que es uno más que uno),
que dejara tu imajen pegada con mi imajen,
mi imajen con tu imajen,
en ascua de fundida plenitud.

Este es el hecho decisivo
de mi imajinación en movimiento,
que yo consideraba un día sobre el mar,
sobre el mar de mi vida y de mi muerte,
el mar de mi esperada solución;
y este es el conseguido
miraje del camino más derecho
de mi ansia destinada.

Por esta maravilla de destino,
entre la selva de mis primaveras,
atraviesa la eléctrica corriente
de la hermosura perseguida mía,
la que volvió, que vuelve y volverá;
la sucesión creciente de mi éstasis de gloria.
Esta es la gloria, gloria solo igual que esta,
la gloria tuya en mí, la gloria mía en ti.

Dios; esta es la suma en canto de los del paraíso
intentado por tanto peregrino.

BY SO MANY PILGRIMS

God-consciousness, you fall upon the world
like a full kiss from a whole face,
in plain satisfaction of all desires.
The midday light
is nothing but your absolute brilliance;
and even the darkest hiding corners
you penetrate with your self,
with the joy of a lofty ownership of life.

To stand over against me
is your natural inclination; and you are
my own open mirror in an immense embrace
(the mirror where one is more than one),
which left your image glued to mine,
my image with your image,
as an ember of fused plenitude.

This is decisive doing
of my imagination in movement,
which I one day visualized upon the sea,
upon the sea of my life and of my death,
the sea of my awaited solution;
and this is the achieved
mirage of the straightest path
of my fateful desire.

Through this wonder of fate,
through this forest of my springtimes,
crosses the electric current
of the beauty I pursued,
the one that returned, returns and will return;
the growing leaps of my ecstasy of glory.
This is the true glory, equal only to this,
the glory of you in me, the glory of me in you.

God, this is the summary, in song, of those
who inhabit paradise, the goal of so many pilgrims.

DE COMPAÑA Y DE HORA

Me despediste, dios, mi pájaro del alba,
del alba de mi alma con cuerpo desvelado,
en la bruma del pálido verdor de primavera;
y estás ahora aquí conmigo, recordándonos,
con tus alas cerradas,
tan contento de haberme matinado
de tu canto de amor al sol primero.

En todo estás a cada hora,
siempre lleno de haber estado lleno,
de haberme a mí llenado de ti mismo,
haberme a mí llenado de mí mismo;
y mi gozo constante de llenarme tú de ti,
es tu vida de dios;
y tu gozo constante de llenarme yo de ti
es mi vida de dios, ¡mi vida, vida!

¡Qué bien se comunican nuestras venas;
por ti circula el sol entre los dos;
circula el sol del mar, el sol del fuego,
el sol del aire, el sol del sol y del amor,
este sol del amor, con el sol de la tierra;
y el amor, el amor solo y todo circula entre los dos,
circula rico, entero, uno entre los dos!

Dios, circula el amor gustador y oloroso,
y cantando circula, tocante y mirador,
porque eres mi flor y mi fruto en mi forma,
porque eres mi espejo en mi idea
(idea, forma, espejo, fruto y flor, y todo único)
porque eres mi música, dios, de todo el mundo,
toda la música de todo el mundo con la nada.

Mi música del pájaro del alba hoy,
ya callado de alba, y distraído
en lo que queda de compaña y de hora,
para todo mi día de confiado estar;
este ir y venir de lo otro a lo mío, de lo mío a lo otro,
contigo, que me esperas siempre, siempre, siempre
con las alas cerradas,
después de todo.

THE COMPANY AND THE HOUR

You said goodbye to me, god, my bird of dawn,
the dawn of my soul and the body in vigil,
in the mist of the pale greenness of spring;
you are here now with me, remembering each other,
with your wings folded,
happy at my early rising
with your song of love at the first light.

You are in everything at every hour,
always filled with having been filled,
of having filled me with yourself;
of having filled me with myself;
and the constant joy of filling me with you
is your life as god;
and your constant joy of my filling up with you
is my life as god, my life, life!

How well our veins communicate;
through you the sun flows between both of us,
the sun of the sea flows, and the sun of fire,
the sun of the air, the sun of the sun and of love,
this sun of love flows with the sun of the earth;
and love, love alone flows and everything else between us,
it flows rich, whole, one between the two of us!

God, make love flow pleasurable and aromatic,
flow singing, touching, glancing,
for you are the flower and fruit in my form,
for you are the mirror in my idea
(idea, form, mirror, fruit and flower, each unique)
for you are my music, god, of the whole world,
the whole music of the whole world plus the nothingness.

Today my music is of the bird of dawn,
with no dawn song, and distracted
in what remains of the company and the hour,
for the rest of my day of faithful waiting;
this coming and going from that other to mine, from mine to that other,
with you, for you wait for me always, always, always
with the wings folded,
beyond everything.

SOY ANIMAL DE FONDO

«En fondo de aire» (dije) «estoy»
(dije), «soy animal de fondo de aire» (sobre tierra),
ahora sobre mar; pasado, como el aire, por un sol
que es carbón allá arriba, mi fuera, y me ilumina
con su carbón el ámbito segundo destinado.

Pero tú, dios, también estás en este fondo
y a esta luz ves, venida de otro astro;
tú estás y eres
lo grande y lo pequeño que yo soy,
en una proporción que es esta mía,
infinita hacia un fondo
que es el pozo sagrado de mí mismo.

Y en este pozo estabas antes tú
con la flor, con la golondrina, el toro
y el agua; con la aurora
en un llegar carmín de vida renovada;
con el poniente, en un huir de oro de gloria.
En este pozo diario estabas tú conmigo,
conmigo niño, joven, mayor, y yo me ahogaba
sin saberte, me ahogaba sin pensar en ti.
Este pozo que era, solo y nada más ni menos,
que el centro de la tierra y de su vida.

Y tú eras en el pozo májico el destino
de todos los destinos de la sensualidad hermosa
que sabe que el gozar en plenitud
de conciencia amadora,
es la virtud mayor que nos trasciende.

Lo eras para hacerme pensar que tú eras tú,
para hacerme sentir que yo era tú,
para hacerme gozar que tú eras yo,
para hacerme gritar que yo era yo
en el fondo de aire en donde estoy,
donde soy animal de fondo de aire

I AM ANIMAL OF DEPTH

"Upon a depth of air" (I said) "I am"
(I said), "I am animal of depth of air" (upon the earth),
now upon the sea; crossing, like the air, through a sun
that is red hot coal up there, my outside, and it lights up
with its hot coals the second fated space.

You, god, are also in this depth
and you see by this light coming from another star;
and you are here and are
the great and the small that I am,
in the exact proportion that is my own,
infinite towards the depth,
the sacred well of myself.

You were here before in this well
with the flower, the swallow, the bull
and the water; with the dawn
in a crimson arrival of renewed life;
with the setting sun in a flight of heavenly gold.
In this daily well you were with me,
with me as a child, young, old, and I was drowning
not knowing you, drowning not thinking of you.
This well, by itself, was no more and no less
than the center of the earth and of life.

You were in the magic well the fate
of all the fates of the beautiful sensuality
that knows that pleasure is plenitude
of loving consciousness,
the greatest virtue that transcends us.

You were so to make me think that you were you,
to make me feel that I was you,
to make me enjoy your being me,
to make me shout that I was I
upon the depth of the air I am standing on,
where I am animal of the depth of air

con alas que no vuelan en el aire,
que vuelan en la luz de la conciencia
mayor que todo el sueño
de eternidades e infinitos
que están después, sin más que ahora yo, del aire.

with wings that do not fly in the air,
but fly in the light of consciousness,
larger than any dreams of eternities and infinities
that arrive, with no more than I have now, later than the air.

II

Dios Deseado
y Deseante

(1949)

II

God Desired
and Desiring

(1949)

LA MENUDA FLORACION

ESTE encuentro del dios que yo decía,
estaba, como en primavera
primera, de menuda floración,
que en este niñodiós que me esperaba:
el mismo niñodiós que yo fui un día,
que dios fue un día en mi Moguer de España;
mi dios y yo que ya soñábamos con este hoy.

                                         Al fin lo tuve.
El sueño no fue sueño, era distancia,
y de ella venía la fragancia,
la fragancia que yo, que dios en niñodiós, los dos
le dimos en botón de primavera.
Ella se dilató y hoy llena un mundo
que yo ensanché para este niñodiós.
   ¡Qué infancia universal, qué yo de dios
de todo el mundo en este niño!

   Tú, mi dios deseado, me guiaste
porque tú lo soñaste también; tú, niñodiós,
eterno niñodiós;
soñaste que por ti yo fuera dios del niño
y niño me dejaste
para que siempre el niño fuera mío.

   ¿Qué alegría mayor
pudo pensar mi sentimiento?
Que no bastaba el puro pensamiento
para pensar al niño; necesario era
crearlo en un florecimiento
de primavera,
en la menuda flor de la ladera,
la flor en luz del puro sentimiento.

   Por eso vive en flor menuda,
en flor del niñodiós, florecilla desnuda,
y en flor del niñodiós desnudo yo lo siento.

THE TINY FLOWERING

This encounter with the god I spoke about,
was, as in a first
spring, of tiny flowering,
for it was in the child-god it waited for me:
the same child-god I was one day myself,
and god too arrived one day in my Moguer of Spain;
my god and I, both already dreaming of this day.

At last I had him,
the dream was not a dream, it was a distance,
and from it the fragrance came,
the fragrance that I, as child-god, that both
gave out in a button of spring.
The fragrance became wider and now it fills the world
I enlarged for that child-god.
What a universal infancy, how much of the I of the god
of the whole world is in that child!

You, my god desired, guided me
for you also dreamt it; you, child-god,
eternal child-god;
you dreamt that for you I would become god in the child
and you left me a child
so that the child could always be mine.

What greater joy could my feeling
ever know?
It was not enough for pure thought
to think the child; it was necessary
to create him in a flowering
of spring,
in the tiny flower by the hillside,
the flower made light by pure feeling.

This is why he lives as a tiny flower,
the child-god flower, naked little flower,
and in that naked flower of the child-god I feel him.

Y EN ORO SIEMPRE LA CABEZA ALERTA

CADA mañana veo la ciudad
donde te hallé del todo, dios, esencia,
conciencia, tú, hermosura llena.
La veo abrirse con la estela verdespuma,
la constante, la limpia estela verdespuma
que me empuja gustosa de tener
espacio y tiempo de venir conmigo;
que me señala persiguiéndome
mi camino seguro de venida. La ciudad . . .

(No, no eran solo polvorientos,
como yo dije, los caminos;
de tan caliente sed y tantas veces;
también del nácar de unas plantas dulces
es el camino de mis pies;
de luz de lo infinito abandonado,
blanco y verde, como un abril del agua,
es su persecución serena.)

. . . En el sinfín abierto, allí, sí, allí,
en un rompiente májico de luces,
está tu despertar, ciudad cruzada
de cruces, largas cruces de ambulancia,
con el ansia de pies, de brazos, manos;
y en sol cardinal siempre la cabeza alerta
a norte, a oeste, a este, a sur,
los cuatro oros de la entrada permanente,
la salida con vuelta.

¡Tu cabeza, ciudad; tus ojos, tus oídos,
tu olfato, con tu tacto y lengua en alma que yo vi,
que yo miré, que olí y oí, toqué, gusté
con emoción seguidamente contenida
de cambio de infinitos!

AND THE HEAD ALWAYS ALERT IN GOLD

I see the city each morning
where I found you whole, god, essence,
consciousness, you, full beauty.
I see it open up with the green trail of foam,
the perennial, the clean foam trail
that pushes me forward in the pleasure of having
space and time arrive with me;
that points out, as it persecutes me,
the sure path of my arrival. The city . . .

(No, they were not only dusty,
as I said, those roads;
so thirsty and so often traversed;
made of mother-of-pearl from sweet plants
is the path of my feet;
made of a light from the abandoned infinite,
white and green, like a watery April,
is its calm persecution.)

. . . On the open endlessness, there, yes, there,
on a magic prism of lights
lies your awakening, city crossed
with crosses, large crosses in ambulances,
searching for feet, arms, hands;
and under the piercing sun the head always alert
towards the north, the west, the east, the south,
the four golden posts of a permanent entrance,
of an exit with a return.

Your head, city; your eyes, your ears,
your nose, your touch and tongue turned into soul as I saw,
as I stared, smelled and heard, tasted with emotion
immediately penetrated
by an exchange of infinites!

LOS PASOS DE LA ENTRAÑA QUE ENCONTRE

EN esta abierta estela vuelan hacia mi fijo estar
y me distienden el corazón tan lleno de verda-
des, los pasos de la entraña que encontré con
mi conciencia deseante del dios bello.

Todos los que sufrieron de esperanza me co-
nocían por la luz ya mía, la luz que el conseguido dios le prende al que más lo desea y la desea.

Por esta estela vienen uno y otro; todos vienen
en brazo inmenso verde y blanco, ese brazo fatal
del que más supo, con un convencimiento definido, de elejir y querer.

THE FOOTSTEPS OF THE WOMB THAT I FOUND

On this open trail, flying towards my fixed being,
extending my heart so full of truths,
I found the footsteps of the womb in my desire
for the beautiful god.

All those who suffered in hope recognized me
by a light already mine, the light that the
achieved god lights up in those who want him
most and desire the light.

On this trail they cross one another; all form
an immense green and white arm, the fateful arm
that belongs to the one who knew the most,
confident of being able to chose and to love.

CHOQUE DE PECHO CON ESPALDA

Eres lo limitado de mi órbita y eres lo ilimitado,
el dentro de mi órbita y el fuera, y lo
hondo y lo estenso; todo lo que yo pude dominar, todo
también lo que yo voy pudiendo.

Y yo sé, y yo sé que un día
alijeraré mi eterno discurrir; y que seré
el andarín sin campanilla,
dominador de todo, a gusto, y, a gusto,
dominando, hasta encontrarme ya conmigo mismo;
choque de pecho con espalda, choque también
de cuerpo y alma, de realidad e imajen.

THE MEETING OF BREAST AND BACK

You are the limits of my orbit and the unlimited,
the inside of my orbit and the outside, and the
depth and the width; all I could control, also
all I could become by wishing.

And I know, and I know that one day I will
slow down my eternal journeying; that I will become
the wanderer without a bell,
in control of all things, feeling at home, and at home
with my control, until I find myself with myself at last;
the meeting place of breast and back, the encounter
of body with soul, of reality with image.

EL CORAZON DE TODO EL CUERPO

Yo fui y vine contigo, dios, entre
aquella pleamar unánime de manos, el olear unánime de brazos; brazos,
   manos,
las ramas del tronco, con raíz de venas,
del corazón de todo el cuerpo, que tú recojes en
tu tierra; y todo en llama, en sombra, en luz, también en
frío; en verde y pardo, en blanco y negro;
en oler, en mirar, en saber, en tocar
y en oír de tantas rayas confundidas.

En gozar de cien rayas confundidas,
yo fui y vine contigo, dios, contigo.

THE HEART OF THE WHOLE BODY

I come and go along with you, god, among the unanimous
high sea of hands, the unanimous waving of arms; arms, hands,
the branches of the trunk with its roots made of veins,
from the heart of the whole body, which you regather in
your land; and all is aflame, in shadows, in light, also in
cold; in green and gray, in white and black;
in smelling, in looking, in knowing, in touching
and in listening to so many entwined lines.

I come and go along with you, god, with you
in enjoying a hundred entwined lines.

RESPIRACION TOTAL DE NUESTRA ENTERA GLORIA

CUANDO sales en sol, dios conseguido,
no estás en el nacerte solo;
estás en el ponerte,
en mi norte, en mi sur;
estás, con los matices de una cara grana,
interior y completa,
que mira para dentro,
en la totalidad del tiempo y el espacio.

Y yo estoy dentro de ella,
dentro de tu conciencia jeneral estoy
y soy tu secreto, tu diamante,
tu tesoro mayor, tu ente entrañable.

Y soy tus entrañas
y en ellas me remuevo
como en aire, y nunca soy tu ahogado;
nunca me ahogaré en tu nido
como no se ahoga un niño en la matriz
de su madre, su dulce nebulosa;
porque tú eres esta sangre mía
y eres su circular,
mi inspiración completa
y mi completa inspiración;
respiración total de nuestra entera gloria.

THE TOTAL BREATH OF OUR ENTIRE GLORY

When you come out as the sun, god achieved,
you are not only in your birth;
you are also in your setting,
in my north, in my south;
you are, with the shades of a sunlit face,
interior and complete,
looking inward,
in the totality of time and space.

And I am in its inside,
I am inside your general consciousness
and I am your secret, your diamond,
your greatest treasure, your loving being.

I am your womb
and within it I move,
as in air, and never drown;
I will never drown in your nest
as a child does not drown
in his mother's womb, his sweet nebula;
for you are my own blood
and you are its flowing,
my complete aspiration
and my complete inspiration;
the total breath of our entire glory.

ESTAS CAYENDO SIEMPRE HASTA MI IMAN

EN mar pasas, en mar acumulado
con todas las bellezas, tú, conseguido dios de la mar,
de mi mar.

Tú eres el sucesivo, lo sucesivo eres;
lo que siempre vendrá, el que siempre vendrá; que
eres el ansia abstracta, la que nunca se fina, porque
el recuerdo tuyo es vida tanto como tú.

Sí; en masa de verdad reveladora, de sucesión
perpetua pasas, en masa de color, de luz,
de ritmo; en densidad de amor estás pasando,
estás viniendo, estás presente siempre;
pasando estás en mí; eres lo ilimitado de mi órbita.

Y me detengo en mi alijeración, porque en el horizonte
del espacio eterno estás cayendo siempre hasta
mi imán. Tu sucesión no es fuga de lo mío,
es venida impetuosa de lo tuyo,
del todo que eres tú, eterno vividor del todo;
caminante y camino a fuerza de
pasado, a fuerza de presente, a fuerza
de futuro.

YOU ARE ALWAYS FALLING TOWARDS MY MAGNET

You cross over the sea, over a sea-like accumulation
of all beauty, you, god achieved from the sea,
from my sea.

You are the becoming, you are what becomes;
what will always come, the one to come always; you
are the abstract desire, the one that never ends, for
the memory of you is as much life as you are.

Yes, you pass in a mass of revealing truth, you
pass in perpetual succession, in a mass of color, of light,
of rhythm; you keep passing in a density of love,
you are living, always present; you are passing in me;
you are the boundlessness of my orbit.

And I linger in my lightness, because from the horizon
of eternal space you keep falling always towards my
magnet. Your continuous passing is not a flight from what is mine,
it is the sudden arriving of what is yours,
of the whole that you are, eternal living of the whole; you
are the journey and the traveller on the strength of the
past, on the strength of the present, on the strength of
the future.

III

Animal de Fondo

y

*Dios Deseado
y Deseante*

(1948–1952)

POEMAS SUELTOS E INEDITOS

III

Animal of Depth

and

God Desired
and Desiring

(1948–1952)

UNPUBLISHED POEMS

ESTOY MIDIENDOME CON DIOS

ENMEDIO de la mar, un barco, este,
sitúa, mide, corta, precisa, relaciona
tu conciencia, la mía, dios.
No vamos por la mar (yo solo con el barco,
mientras los otros duermen)
vamos por tu conciencia, que es ahora
redonda, gris, lluviosa, acojedora,
como yo mismo, dios, ahora.

   Esta es la noche igual a aquella
de mi partida, la de la pureza
del mar, mar de igual ola,
aquella de la puerta de la luna
a la que se llegaba por su propia estela,
luna velada hoy por la cortina de tu lluvia.

Vamos, dios, por conciencia
de agua total en hilos de arpa de alta música,
con acompañamiento de honda densidad moral.

   Y enmedio de la mar, tu jeometría
surje de pronto, te sitúa,
mide, corta, precisa, relaciona
conmigo y en tu barco que vijilo;
barco que parte en tres mi vida:
una vida en el este,
otra en el sur, otra en el norte;
y yo sereno enmedio de la mar de oeste,
lleno de amor,
el centro de la rosa de las lluvias del amor.

   Lleno de amor, el mío, un barco
y yo, el amor enmedio del amor,
de tanto amor que necesita el mar
para medirte, dios.

   Y enmedio de la mar yo estoy midiéndote,
enmedio de la mar y en este barco, este,
estoy midiéndome contigo, dios.

I AM MEASURING MYSELF WITH GOD

In the middle of the sea, a ship, this one,
places, measures, cuts up, fixes, relates to
your consciousness, mine, god.
We are not crossing the sea (I alone with the ship
while all the others sleep)
we are crossing your consciousness, which now is
round, gray, rainy, welcoming,
as I am myself, god, now.

This night is identical to the one
of my departure, the one
with the pure sea, sea of even waves,
night of the gate of the moon
that one could reach climbing its trail,
moon today covered with a curtain of rain.

We are crossing, god, a consciousness
of total water in harp strings of high music,
with the accompaniment of a deep moral density.

But in the middle of the sea suddenly
your geometry appears, it places you,
it measures you, it cuts up, fixes, relates
to me and your ship I keep watch over;
this ship breaks my life in three:
one life to the east,
one to the south, another to the north,
and I in the middle, calm in the sea of the west,
filled with love,
the center of a rose made of rains of love.

Full of love, my own, a ship
and I, love in the center of love,
of so much love as the sea needs
to measure you, god.

In the middle of the sea I am measuring you,
in the middle of the sea and of this ship, this one;
I am measuring you with me, god.

EL MAR INMENSO

(Prosa)

No es roja, pero tiene rojo ardor esta noche de luna con mi dios; y las olas son llama sin ser rojas. Un fuego interno la traspasa y traspasa y trasluce su estela, caminante detrás de mi camino seguidor, caminante delante de su amante.

La luna ¿es la conciencia, deseante también de lo distante que se acerca para tenerme mi diamante?

Conciencia en baja luna, deseante conciencia de lo distante, ahora que se acerca por no dejar de ver el sol de mi diamante.

Diamante de verdad es el que tengo esta noche en mi vida, noche de gran verano hacia mi invierno. Se me acerca la llama conseguida, la llama conocida, la llama consentida, del lejos que se va quedando, que se va borrando.

Y este ardor ¿no es su vida, no es mi vida, no es la vida que se viene conmigo por el cielo, para ganar mi paso por el suelo del agua, a acompañarme mi desvelo con sed de corazón, reconocida?

Bien penetrado vengo del cariño de lo que yo prendí con mi presencia. Yo le puse en su flor una vehemencia tan grande, mi conciencia de niño; y ello me tiene y quiere con fulgor también de niño; fulgor de niño en seno grande, sol, conversión del amor impetuoso en fuente de mirífica inocencia. Inocencia, esa agua que es demencia en inmanencia que pasa y que traspasa la existencia y la renueva con rubor intenso.

Por dios viene a mi amor la luna en mar inmenso.

THE IMMENSE SEA

(Prose)

It is not red, but tonight with the moon and my god it feels burning red; and the waves are flames, though they are not red. An inner fire penetrates and penetrates and turns its trail into light, journey-moon following my following trail, a traveller following his lover.

The moon, is it consciousness desiring what is distant coming closer to hold my diamond?

Consciousness when the moon is low, consciousness desiring the distant, now approaching not to lose sight of the sun of my diamond.

A true diamond is what I have tonight in my life, the night of a large summer facing winter. The achieved flame is coming closer, the known flame, the accepted flame, from the far away that is left behind and fades.

And this burning, is it not her life, is it not mine, is it not life coming along with me through the sky, in order to step ahead of me on the floor of the water, to accompany my vigil in a thirst of hearts, rediscovered?

I come fully penetrated by the love of what I stole with my presence. I desired its flower so intensely, with my consciousness of a child; it has me and loves me too with the radiance of a child; the radiance of a child within a large womb, sun, transformation of uncontrolled love into a fountain of transparent innocence. Innocence, the water with madness beneath it crossing and crisscrossing our existence and transforming it with intense flashes.

Through god the moon comes to my love upon an immense sea.

EN ORDEN DE HERMOSURA

Los monstruos del crepúsculo nocturno
se salen de un crepúsculo más alto,
pululan por el cielo marino, y bajan
con todos los reflejos del sol morado y grana
en sus ojos de abismo.

Entre ellos estamos,
dios, y tu mano con la mía
acarician sus lomos
que redondea el tiempo del espacio.

Esa es también nuestra familia,
en nuestra casa tienen su guarida,
y cuando salen por la tarde,
ya encerrados los de las horas claras
esparcen la grandeza
que el misterio les pone en sus entrañas.

Son los entendedores del misterio;
misterio son quizá para los otros
mas no para nosotros que sabemos
que podemos abrir y entrar los dos en él
y amar en él a lo que en él se acoje.

Que podemos amar
monstruos amados
estos seres de nuestra semejanza
entre los cuales va nuestra conciencia,
dios, como el más pastor,
igualándolos
a nosotros en orden de hermosura.

IN THE ORDER OF BEAUTY

The monsters of the evening twilight
come out from a higher twilight,
swarming through the nautical sky, descending
with the reflections of a mauve and red sun
in their abysmal eyes.

We are among them,
god, and your hand with mine
caresses their flanks
that the time of space has rounded.

They are also our family,
they make our home their lair,
and when they come out in the evening,
those that roam in the clear hours already locked up,
they spread the grandeur
that mystery has bestowed on their wombs.

They are those who understand the mystery;
a mystery, perhaps, to others
but not to us who know
that they inhabit a dominion
we are able to open and enter together
and love what has found protection there.

We are able to love
loved monsters,
those beings in our likeness
among which our consciousness moves,
god, the best shepherd,
making them equal
to us in the order of beauty.

DE UN OASIS ETERNO DE LO INTERNO

(Estar despierto yo ¡qué maravilla!
ANTES)

EL venir es un dios, mi Dios, y yo le cojo
las formas más humanas a su esencia,
en un ansia de amor que es vivir mío.

Me está llamando siempre
en los hermosos espejismos
que el ocaso nos abre en tierra y mar,
fondo tras fondo del oriente eterno;
y en ese juego, en ese fuego
de fondos superpuestos
que siguen en las noches para mí,
está la maravilla de mi despertar.
¡Estar despierto yo! ¡qué maravilla!

La maravilla de mi despertar es esa,
un llegar de un viaje de viajes,
un pasar de occidentes como vidrios
que se van despegando eternamente
para que yo les vea
su entera desnudez de forma y vida.
Y en todos está dios de mil maneras,
en todos está el sueño de este dios
que yo fabrico de la gloria con mis noches,
coronas planetarias de mis días,
coronas de los días de mis días.

Sucesión de coronas es mi dios,
coronas que coronan solo un centro
que es un ojo, es un ver,
un sí mismo tan yo, maravilloso yo,
que mi aurora no es más que la sonrisa
de haberme dado a luz yo mismo
de mi sueño, mi sueño.

Mi amor de cada noche,
mi sol de cada día,
mi venir, mi venir, venir, venir mi Dios,

FROM AN ETERNAL OASIS OF THE INTERIOR

"I, to be awake, what a marvel!"

The future is a god, my God, and I steal
from him the most human forms of his essence,
in a desire to love, which for me is my life.

But he is always calling
from the beautiful reflections
that the sunsets open up for us over earth and sea,
depth upon depth of the eternal east;
and in that game, that flame
of superimposed depths
following one another in the night for me,
comes the miracle of waking up.
I, to be awake, what a marvel!

The marvel of my awakening is this,
to arrive from a journey of journeys,
to cross west upon west like mirrors
that come unglued eternally
so that I may watch
the total nudity of shape and life.
And in each god there are a thousand shapes,
in each there is a dream of each god
that I build out of the glory of my nights,
planetary crowns of my days,
crowns of the days of my days.

A succession of crowns is my god,
crowns crowning only one center
that is an eye, a way of seeing,
a self so much my own I, my marvellous I,
for my dawn is no more than the smile
at having given birth to myself by myself
out of my dreams, my dreams.

My love of every night,
my sun of every day,
my future, my future, future future God,

DE UN OASIS ETERNO DE LO INTERNO (*continuación*)

mi porvenir constante en que mi día entero
es el gozar de un sueño conseguido,
de un oasis eterno de lo interno,
este gozar de ver ¡con qué descanso lleno!
la verdad,
que será más verdad cada mañana.

my constant future where my whole day
is the constant pleasure of a dream achieved,
of an eternal oasis of the interior,
this pleasure of witnessing, filled with so much rest!
the truth
that will become more true every morning.

EL OLEAR DEL MEDIODIA CANTA

En un tremor de bronce derretido, unánime
ascua blanca y ondeante, el olear del mediodía
canta hacia arriba, con verde y contenido hervor,
tu regreso conmigo,
dios conseguido,
mi regreso contigo,
al lugar donde tú te me fijaste.

Me lo fijaste tú; y yo no supe lo que era el
milagro, hasta que tú te me metiste dentro o me
metiste en ti; y yo fui dios seguro de ti mismo
seguro de mí mismo
y tú, seguro de mí mismo y de ti mismo,
dios.
Tú me significaste la belleza que yo canté y
conté que era una belleza verdadera y siempre
venidera:
la belleza que yo te había designado,
dios deseante y deseado,
como dios de mi vida conseguida; que tú estabas
conmigo y que el mundo, contigo, era mi amigo.

Presente estás en mar ardiente en movimiento;
y todas las bellezas del presente me las das con
tus ojos, que pasan a mis manos la plenitud
serena universal.

THE WAVES OF MIDDAY SING

With a thunder of melted bronze, a unanimous
ember all white and waving, the midday surf
sings upwards, with a green and contained boiling,
your return with me,
my return with you,
to the space where you fixed yourself in me,
god achieved.

You fixed it yourself; and I did not know
what kind of miracle it was, until you penetrated
me or penetrated me in you; and I became god
sure of you, sure of me
and you, sure of me and of you,
god.

You pointed out to me the beauty that I sang and
told, it was a beauty of truth and always
to come:
the beauty I had framed for you,
god desiring and desired,
as the god of the life I achieved; that you were
with me and that the world, with you, was my friend.

You are present in this burning, moving sea;
and all the beauties of the present you give
to me with your eyes, surrender to my hands
the calm, universal plenitude.

CON UN SELLO QUE NO CIERRA

Por esta negra noche de la mar,
vamos para las otras ciudades de la tierra,
en donde los estraños, dios, ya nos conocen
y se abren de brazos
y nos abren queriendo nuestros brazos.

¡Qué gloria de hermosura,
qué abrir de brazos y de corazones,
del animal, del hombre y de dios
quien les forma en sus bocas esa rosa en punto,
que es el abierto beso!

El beso es la conciencia del amor.
Por el beso fundimos nuestros cuerpos
con sustancia de alma;
el beso es esta gracia que nos sella
a todos con un sello que no cierra,
que nos abre lo mismo que una llave.

Llave del mundo, beso
que abre también la noche de la mar,
si abrazamos la mar y la besamos
con sentido de astro;
estrellación de todo el mundo,
besos constelados
en armonía de presencia de diamante
de mina eterna descubierta.

WITH A SEAL THAT DOES NOT SEAL

Through this dark night of the sea,
we travel to the other cities of the earth,
where strangers, god, already know us
and open their arms
and open ours wanting our embraces.

What glory of beauty,
what an opening up of hearts and arms,
from animals, men, and god
who shape in their mouths this ready rose,
an open kiss!

A kiss is the consciousness of love.
Through a kiss we melt our bodies
with the substance of the soul;
a kiss is the gift that seals us all
with a seal that does not seal,
which opens us up just like a key.

Key of the world, kiss that also
opens the night of the sea,
if we embrace the sea and kiss it
with the feeling of a star;
the whole world becomes stars
with kisses in constellations
of a harmony of diamonds
from a mine eternally discovered.

TUS DOS OJOS, MIS DOS MANOS

Este mar es el mar
que yo crucé ya quince veces,
solo que hoy es ya mar tuyo en mí,
no el mar de mi bregar, de mi esperar contigo,
no el mar que yo te dije
que era movimiento y cambio eternizado,
sino este mar que yo he creado
a mi imajen y semejanza tuyas,
dios deseado y deseante;
el mar que yo con mi esperanza cautivé
en cautiverio de una fe de amargor dulce.

Y ya nadie podrá
sacarme de esta fe mas que esta otra
en que las olas de este otro cielo
alzan su fondo hasta su límite;
este mar donde están como en las nubes,
donde tú y yo nos encontramos en mi hogar,
seguros de que somos los hermanos,
que somos los humanos, dos humanos, dos hermanos,
como son dos tus ojos,
dos mis manos.

YOUR EYES ARE TWO AND MY HANDS ARE TWO

This sea is the sea
I have already crossed fifteen times,
only that today it is already your sea in me,
and not the sea of my labor, of my waiting with you;
not the sea I mentioned that
was movement and change eternalized,
but the sea I have created,
according to my image and the likeness of you,
god desired and desiring;
the sea I seduced with my hope
while exiled in a sweet and bitter faith.

And no one will be able
to move me from this faith except the other one
where the waves of that other sky
raise their depths up to its boundaries;
that sea where they dwell as in the clouds,
where you and I met in my home;
surely we are brothers,
surely we are humans, two humans, two brothers,
just as your eyes are two
and my hands are two.

EL ALMA AHORA DE LA LUZ

CONTIGO voy, dios, en lo más gris.
Contigo voy conmigo.
Igual me es la luz ilimitada,
los oros con azules,
que esta luz lloviznante de la nube entera.

   No hay contigo penumbra
(la sombra es tan hermosa,
que tiene igual diamante que tu sol).
No hay penumbra contigo.
La penumbra es un alma de alma, y me parece
el alma ahora de la luz.

   El alma de la luz eres si eres
la luz del alma, dios de la belleza.

THE SOUL NOW OF LIGHT

I walk with you, god, in the ultimate gray.
With you I walk with myself.
It is the same to me to be under a limitless light,
or under the golds with blues,
or under this rainy light of a whole cloud.

There is no shade with you
(the shade is so beautiful,
it owns the same diamond as your sun).
There is no shade with you.
The shade is the soul of a soul, and appears to me now
to be the soul of light.

You are the soul of light if you are
the light of the soul, god of beauty.

LA LUZ QUE ALUMBRA POR DEBAJO EL SUEÑO

IGUAL, tú sales, dios, en todas partes,
el sol, también, de la mañana;
y saliendo me haces salir a mí,
y tú y yo, los deseados deseantes,
somos en todas partes como el sol,
igual que el sol, igual que el sol:
conciencia rosabella de la aurora,
conciencia blancabella del cenit,
conciencia rojabella del poniente.

Tú y yo, e igual que el primer sol, lo vemos todo,
desde nuestro salir;
todo lo levantamos
con nuestra luz sola de amor
rosa por la mañana,
blanca en el mediodía,
roja a la tarde.

Y asi la . . . en la noche.
deslumbramiento hondo del alma
que recibe la luz de otro hemisferio,
la luz que alumbra el sueño por debajo.

THE LIGHT THAT ILLUMINES OUR DREAMS FROM BELOW

You come out evenly, god, everywhere,
a sun, also, in the morning;
and coming out you force me out,
and you and I, the desired desiring,
stand everywhere like the sun,
just as the sun, just as the sun;
rosebeautiful consciousness of the dawn,
whitebeautiful consciousness of the zenith,
redbeautiful consciousness of the sunset.

You and I, just as the first sun, witness everything,
from the moment of our rising;
we lift up everything
with just our light of love,
pink in the morning,
white at midday,
red in the evening.

And thus the . . . in the night,
deep dazzle of the soul
that receives light from another hemisphere,
the light that illumines our dreams from below.

DE MI AUSENCIA EN PRESENCIA

ESTE diamante grana que tengo yo tan dentro,
dios deseado y deseante,
este hondo, fiel, esperador diamante
que mi sangre encarmina y hace flor constante
con todas las riquezas de su riego de luz,
ha aumentado, creciendo en mis entrañas
minadas por tu ansia y mi ansia cavadoras;
y es hoy tan grande como el de un ciego ya total,
tan grande como un universo ciego.

Y un ciego soy de tanta deslumbrancia
de fe con mi esperanza, mi caridad en torno;
pero puedo más verme como en sueños tuyos,
en mi lodo. Este lodo amasado por mí con tu donancia,
hasta sacarle esa fragancia
que se quema, alma mía, en la luz limpia
de mi diamante, flor diamante
que encarmina mi sangre.

¡Rosa diamante que me llena, que me emplena
hasta estas playas mías, mi litoral, mi costa
ante el mar que es el mundo!
Ya es bastante mi ser para ser mundo
continente de ti, limpia conciencia,
conciencia, dios, tú mío;
este diamante, este diamante, este diamante
que mi sangre encarmina
hasta hacerme absoluta de videncia
la ceguera en deslumbre
de mi ausencia en presencia.

FROM MY ABSENCE INTO A PRESENCE

This scarlet diamond I hold so deep within,
god desired and desiring,
this deep, faithful, waiting diamond
that my blood turns red to make a constant flower
with all the riches of its irrigations of light,
has enlarged, grown in my insides
mined through desire for you and my digging desire;
and today it is as large as that of one totally blind,
as large as a blind universe.

Blind I am from so much dazzling
faith in my hope and in my love all around;
but I can see myself better as though in your dreams,
in my dust. This dust made mud by me through your gifts,
until I was able to extract this scent
which burns, my soul, from the clean light
of my diamond, diamond-flower
that turns my blood red.

Diamond-rose that fills me, that enlarges one
to reach those beaches of mine, my shore, my coast
facing the sea that is the world!
It is sufficient for me to be a world
containing you, clean consciousness,
consciousness, god, you my own;
this diamond, this diamond, this diamond
that turns red with my blood
until I become able to see
through the dazzled blindness
of my absence into a presence.

UN ASCUA DE CONCIENCIA Y DE VALOR

Tú prendes con tu sol fuego a mi día,
dios, y así todo comienza a prepararse en ti
para este gran incendio que la aurora,
antigua levantada de la vida,
determina gritando su alegror
porque tú, dios y yo nos fusionemos
en este comenzar de comenzares.

La llama se levanta y se derrama
con humo negro aún del nochear;
y luego el humo blanco se disipa
y va quedando este dorar unánime
del diamante total de mi universo.
Todo quiere fundirse en este fuego
en el que yo, presente, me fundí
desde el grito primero de la aurora.

Un ascua hemos de ser en plenitud
los dos, dios deseado y deseante,
de vida deslumbrada y deslumbrante;
un ascua de conciencia y de valor;
y, como con la noche nos perdimos
en la nada más dulce de tu todo,
con el día nos hemos de encontrar
en el todo más hondo de tu nada.

AN EMBER OF CONSCIOUSNESS AND VALOR

You light my day with the fire of your sun,
god, and thus all begins to get ready in you
with this large fire that the dawn,
earliest riser of life,
frames by shouting her joy
so that you, god, and I become one
in this beginning of all beginnings.

The flame rises and spreads
still carrying the black smoke of night;
then the white smoke fades
and this unanimous gold remains
out of the total diamond of my universe.
Everything wants to melt in that fire
where I am present, melted already
at the first cry of the dawn.

We must become a burning ember in plenitude,
the two of us, god desired and desiring,
of dazzled and dazzling life;
an ember of consciousness and valor;
and since with the night we became lost
in the nothingness of your all,
we must find each other with the day
and in the great depth of your nothingness.

TU, SECRETO FILON, ROSADIAMANTE

DIOS, tú te me ofreciste abierto
del todo para mí, como la rosa
que siempre supe, de que siempre hablé
sin saber cómo era antes que tú
le abrieras el sentido para mí.
Y en sentido de rosa yo viví,
como en un sueño realizado,
días y noches, por la mar, contigo.

¿De pronto, ahora te me cierras
otra vez? ¿Un invierno me preparas
sin ti, sol de esta baja vida?
¿Te has ido a otro, dios, a referirle,
como a mí me has estado refiriendo,
la suprema verdad de mi conciencia?

¿Ahora el aire, el fuego, el agua,
la tierra y el amor serán estéril
desierto gris cerrado para el ansia?

No, no, yo sé que eso no es,
yo sé que ahora estás dormido;
yo sé que cada uno en sí te encuentra
diferente; que no eres tú dos veces,
de dos maneras, sino uno en uno,
sino uno ¡y no más! en cada uno.
Yo solo te he vivido, te he tenido,
te he abierto, rosadiós, dios en la rosa
que siempre supe, de que siempre hablé
sin saber cómo era antes que tú
le abrieras el sentido para mí.

Sí, yo lo sé, lo sé cerrado dios,
cerrado dios ahora y dentro de mí solo,
en la mina que tienes dentro de mí solo,
tú, secreto filón, rosadiamante.

YOU, SECRET GOLD MINE, DIAMONDROSE

God, you offered yourself fully open
to me, like a rose
I had always known, of which I spoke always
not knowing how it was before you
opened up its meaning to me.
With the meaning of this rose I lived
a dream achieved,
nights and days, on the sea, with you.

Then suddenly, did you close yourself
up again? Are you readying a winter
without you for me, sun of this base life?
Have you gone to someone else, god, to whisper
to him, as you have been whispering to me,
the supreme truth of my consciousness?

Now the air, the fire, the water,
the earth, even love will become barren
desert, gray and closed to my desire!

No, no, I know this is not so,
I know you are now sleeping,
I know each one finds you within himself,
though different; that you are not you twice,
in two different ways, but one in one,
only one and no more! in each one
I have lived you only, have held you only,
have opened you only, rosegod, god in the rose
I always knew, of whom I always spoke
not knowing how it was before you
revealed its meaning to me.

Yes, I know, I know, hermetic god,
god now closed only within myself
in the mine you own within me only,
you, secret gold mine, diamondrose.

EN UN NIDO DE ENTRAÑA

Muchos pedazos de mi fantasía
arden serenos, lentos en el espejismo
de esas ciudades que se continúan
indefinidamente y pasan a la noche
en la última raya del mar dorado o gris,
como nido de entraña.

El sol, la lluvia, el vendaval, la bruma,
los regazan y alivian
allí y aquí y a un tiempo mismo,
con calidez de amor a un deseante dios
de esta entraña de nido.

Ni en mí ni en ella
se pierde ese gozar de abrigo suave.
¿Cómo podré alejarme,
si estos pedazos de mi vida permanecen
con realidad sencilla en él, ese espejismo?
No, no podré alejarme porque me he quedado
en un nido de entraña.

Nido de primavera sola, una conciencia
anidada por dios en lugar justo,
lugar para vivida complaciente y complacida,
lugar del suceder de lo vivido,
para pasar de lo vivido,
con entraña de nido.

IN A NEST WITHIN A WOMB

Many parts of my fantasy burn serenely,
slowly, within the mirage
of these cities that follow each other
indefinitely and pass on to the night
in the last line of the sea, golden or gray,
like a nest within a womb.

The sun, the rain, the wind, the foam
welcome them and soothe them
there and here and at the same time,
with the warmth of love for a desiring god
within this nest in a womb.

Neither in me nor in her
does one lose the joy of a soft shelter.
How will I be able to go away,
if these pieces of my life remain
simply held in a mirage?
No, I will not be able to go away for I have found
a nest within a womb.

A nest of spring alone, a consciousness
nestled by god in the exact place,
a place for a complacent and complaisant life,
for the passing of the lived life,
for the passing of the lived life
with the womb of a nest.

EN DINAMISMO DE ESPRESION GLORIOSA

ENORMES perrosnubes negros ladran
por todo el horizonte de poniente
en prodijiosa algarabía de adiós loco,
a la ciudad en ascuas que el crepúsculo
deshace poco a poco en su alto abismo.

Ladran a los colores rojos, pardos;
a tus colores, dios, a los colores
de tu coronación (de mi coronación) nocturna;
a los colores de tu casa,
a tus colores sin más nombre ni destino
que la belleza presente, oscura o clara;
belleza sucesiva
clara u oscura, que es lo mismo
para la compenetración de nuestra gracia.

Tú mismo te contienes conteniéndome,
¡Qué lengua milagrosa
la que el sol, ya de noche, les levanta
a estos perros de nubes;
qué lengua de unidad
que a ti y a mí nos hacen, como a ellos
gritar de amor, de gloria, de alegría
gritar también de gozo oscuro!

¡Qué lengua relijiosa
en la que el perro y tú y yo nos confundimos
en dinamismo de espresión gloriosa!

A MOVEMENT OF GLORIOUS EXPRESSION

Enormous, black, dogclouds bark
along the whole western horizon
in a prodigious uproar of mad goodbyes,
to the city in burning embers that the sunset
slowly unravels in its high abyss.

They bark at the red, gray colors;
at your colors, god, the colors
of your coronation (my coronation) at night
at the colors of your home,
at your colors with no other name or destiny
than the present beauty, dark or clear;
succeeding beauty
dark or clear, which is the same
in the intermingling of our grace.

You contain yourself by restraining me,
what a miraculous tongue
the sun, night having fallen, raises
in those cloud dogs;
what a tongue of unity
which forces you and me, like them,
to shout of love, of glory, of joy,
to shout also of dark joy!

What a religious tongue
where the dog and you and I become one
within a movement of glorious expression!

LA TIERRA DE LOS TERRENALES

GRACIAS, mi dios de todas las ventanas,
mi conciencia en belleza, de todas las ventanas
que me entran esa vida
que tanto amo;
ese calor de sangre circulante
en cuerpos con un alma que me quieren,
me miran dulces, me sonríen lentos,
me hablan cariñosos,
en este nido natural.

Ahora estoy rodeado,
como el enamorado pájaro, de flores,
en su amor palpitante,
de seres que trabajan en el centro
de la naturaleza convivida,
repartida en presencia y en figura,
tocada (por la mano) en su secreto,
descifrada en su rica confusión,
amada en vida y muerte.

Este es el íntimo preludio
de la entrada del resto, de mi resto
(lo que voy dejando; con mi quema
de ilusión fervorosa) en el rescoldo,
(como la hoja seca separada en humo,
en recuerdo y ceniza)
que luego irá apagando en su regazo
la tierra de los terrenales,
que nos rodeará a los dos
con su ternura y con su simpatía.

THE LAND OF EARTHLY QUESTS

Thanks, god of all my windows,
my consciousness in beauty, for all those windows
that bring me this life
I love so much;
the heat of the flowing blood
in bodies with a soul that loves me,
that looks at me sweetly, smiles at me slowly,
speaks to me softly
in this natural nest.

Now I am surrounded,
like a bird in love by flowers
palpitating with love,
by creatures working at the center of
nature communally lived,
shared through presence and figure,
touched (by the hand) in its secret,
deciphered in its rich confusion,
loved in life and death.

This is the intimate prelude
of the coming of all the rest, the rest of my own
(what I keep leaving by burning
feverish illusions) in embers,
(like the dry leaf dissolved in smoke,
in memory and ashes)
whose fire will become extinguished in her lap,
the lap of the land of earthly quests
which surrounds the two of us
with its tenderness and its sympathy.

DIOS, SOL ENTRE LOS ARBOLES

GRACIAS, dios deseante, aurora grana,
dios, sol entre los árboles cobrizos de este hoy,
de este otro diciembre triunfador,
granador de la entraña comarcana,
de toda la comarca de este mundo.

El sol quemó la noche
como un centro encendido,
y el amor misterioso
se concierta en amor resplandeciente.

Tu corazón, sol, dios, es lo que quema,
y el sol ¡al fin! se llama corazón de dios.

GOD, SUN AMONG THE TREES

Thank you, god desiring, red dawn,
god, sun among the copper trees of this today,
of this again triumphant December,
ripening god of the early womb,
of the whole earth of this world.

The sun burned the night
like a flaming center,
and now mysterious love
is transformed into resplendent love.

Your heart, sun, god, is what burns,
and the sun, at last! is called the heart of god.

ESTE DIA QUE ES TODA LA VIDA

ME estabas esperando en este oro
que la mañana entra por el oto
de mis olmos de otoño (un ala inmensa
que se posa en el tronco más recóndito)
para decirme, cálido y sereno,
que hay que vivir en oro todo el día.

Este día que es toda la vida.

THIS DAY THAT IS THE WHOLE OF MY LIFE

You were waiting for me within this gold
that the morning brings from the hill
of my elms in autumn (an immense wing
resting on the most hidden trunk)
to tell me, warm and serene,
that one must live in gold the whole day.

This day that is the whole of my life.

EN LO DESNUDO DE ESTE HERMOSO FONDO

Quiero quedarme aquí, no quiero irme
a ningún otro sitio.
              Todos los paraísos
(que me dijeron) en que tú habitabas,
se me han desvanecido en mis ensueños
porque me comprendí mejor este en que vivo,
ya centro abierto en flor de lo supremo.

Verdor de primavera de mi atmósfera,
¿qué luz podrá sacar de otro verdor
una armonía de totalidad más limpia,
una gloria más grande y fiel de fuera y dentro?

Esta fue y es y será siempre
la verdad:
tu oído, visto, comprendido en este paraíso mío,
tú de verdad venido a mí
en lo desnudo de este hermoso fondo.

IN THE NAKEDNESS OF THIS BEAUTIFUL DEPTH

I wish to remain here, I do not wish to move
to any other place.
All the paradises (they spoke to me about)
which you inhabited,
have disappeared in my dreams
for I was able to understand better the one I live in,
this one, now a center opened
in flower to the highest.

The green of spring in the air is all around me,
what light will be able to bring out from some other green
a harmony more totally clear,
a glory greater and more faithful from the outside or inside?

This was and is and will always be
the truth:
your ear, seen, understood in this my paradise,
you, who truly came to me
in the nakedness of this beautiful depth.

EL DESNUDO INFINITO

(Prosa)

No, dios, no me deslumbres con relumbres, que yo no quiero que esta costumbre recargada de historia acumulada dé relumbre. Déjame con mis ojos en lo mío, déjame con mi fuego del sol, mi sol de cada día, carbón y luz de cada hora; con la luz de mi hierba verde; con el ansia de lo que quiero contener y retener en mi mirada.

No quiero exaltación de las eternidades, quiero mi exaltación para llegar a las eternidades de mi día que corona la noche con su nada en sueño; esa distancia quiero que es la noche, porque sin noche nada empieza, y yo quiero volver, volver, volver.

Me gusta esta distancia, fiel conciencia, en la que puedo realizar lo que yo soy y quiero; me basta con la eternidad de una mirada que dé su eternidad, y con el horizonte que esa mirada mía atrae con su imán. Entre horizonte y ojo, está la eternidad que yo decía, el momento, el momento de eternidad que tanto hice y quise; mis arenales, mis únicas eternidades. (Eternidad y no eternismo, la palabra huera de los aficionados al teatro eterno.)

La eternidad es solo lo que concibo yo de eternidad, con todos mis sentidos dilatados; la eternidad que quiero yo es esta eternidad de aquí, y de aquí con ella, más que en ella, porque yo quiero, dios, que tú te vengas a mi espacio, al tiempo que yo te he limitado en lo infinito, a lo que es hoy en lo infinito, a lo que tú eres de infinito; al fin de tanto vuelo en lo imposible.

Quiero tu nombre, dios, orijen nada más y fin; y no fin como término, sino como propósito. Quiero, nombrado dios, que tú te hagas por mi amor esto que soy, un ente, un ser, un hombre, y en una atmósfera de hombre, de lo que el nombre hombre significa (hombre con la mujer que significa el nombre de mujer; los dos en uno, en una; y tu conciencia hermosa en ese uno de los dos entre los dos).

Amor de cada día y pan de cada día y luz de cada día; y sombra y paz de cada noche; dos infinitos conseguidos, y todo hacia el futuro, al fin que dije tanto. Que la atmósfera tuya quiera situar, con una luz o un fuego de aureola, cierta aureola no pintada, significando tu infinito; el infinito solo, el infinito limpio, el desnudo infinito que puedo conseguir de ti y de mí.

55

THE NAKED INFINITE

(Prose)

No, god, do not dazzle me with dazzling lights, for I do not wish to become the custom of a history encumbered with dazzling lights. Let me stay with my eyes on what is mine, let me stay with the fire of my sun, my daily sun, coal and light of my every hour; with the light of my green grass; with the desire of what I am able to retain and contain in my gaze.

I do not wish the exultation of eternities, I long for my own exultation to reach the eternities of my day that crown the nights with their nothingness of dreams; I long for that distance, the night, for without the night nothing begins, and I long to return, return, return.

I like this distance, faithful consciousness, where I am able to realize what I am and desire; the eternity of one look that gives out its own eternity is enough for me, and the horizon that my own look attracts with its own magnet. Between horizon and eye lies the eternity I mentioned, the moment, the moment of eternity which so many times I made and desired; the desires of my flesh are my only eternity. (Eternity but not eternalism, the empty word of those in love with the theatre of eternities.)

Eternity is what I myself am able to conceive of eternity with all my senses expanded; the eternity I long for is the eternity of here, of here with it, rather than in it, for I long for you, god, to move into my space, the time I have limited for you in the infinite, what of today is in the infinite, what you are of the infinite; at the end of so much flying in the impossible.

I want your name, god, only as origin and end; not an end like a terminal, but a project. I want, named god, that you become for my love what I am, a being, someone being, a man, within the context of man, what the name man means (man with woman which means the name of woman; both in one, s/he; and your beautiful consciousness in the one made of two, between two).

Love and bread of everyday and light of everyday; shadow and peace of every night; two infinites achieved, both facing the future, towards the end I mentioned. I wish for your orbit to place, with a halo or light or fire, some other halo not painted by anyone else symbolizing your infinity; infinity by itself, the clear infinity, the naked infinity that I am able to achieve from you and from me.

121

UN DIOS EN BLANCO

Como en el infinito, Dios,
vuelvo a tu orijen (tu orijen que es mi fin)
y quizá a tu fin, sin nada de ese enmedio
que las jentes te han puesto encima
de tu sola, tu limpia luz.

   Y yo no necesito en mí que tú, Dios, seas
ese dechado nulo
que millones de manos,
sin saber lo que hacían, te bordaron,
por modelo, en un cáñamo
que fue limpio, fue limpio.

                              Una blanca hoja,
reflejo de una mente en blanco,
eres tú para mí, y en ella tú palpitas
con color de mi tiempo, desde aquel niñodiós
que en mi Moguer de España fui yo un día,
hasta este niñodiós que quiero otra vez ser
para morir, el nuevo siempre;
el que el niño comprende como niño,
sin interés ninguno,
como en el infinito, Dios, nuestro infinito.

   Yo te puedo cargar con copa plena,
como el árbol del fruto que ya soy,
que yo quisiera descargar y que descargo.

   Pero ¿te he de cargar con mano vieja?
No, no, yo soy el niño último,
tú un Dios en blanco eres;
y no te cargaré con mano impura.

   (¡Yo no te descargué con mano impura!)

A BLANK GOD

As in the infinite, God,
I return to your origin (your origin that is my end)
and may be your end, with nothing in between,
the between people have placed over
your one and limpid light.

I do not need you God to become
my useless exemplar
that millions of hands,
not knowing what they were doing, embroidered,
as a model upon a canvas
that was clean, was clean.

A white page,
mirror of a blank mind
you are to me and in it you palpitate
with the color of my time, from the child-god
that in my Moguer of Spain I was one day,
to this child-god I wish to become again
in order to die, always a new one;
the one the child understands as a child,
with no attachments
as in the infinite, God, our infinite.

I can fill you with a full cup,
like a tree with the fruit I already am,
which I wish to unload and that I unload.

But, am I going to load you with an old hand?
No, no, I am the last child,
you a blank God;
and I will not load you with an impure hand.

(I did not unload you with an impure hand!)

SI LA BELLEZA INMENSA ME RESPONDE O NO

BUSCÁNDOTE como te estoy buscando,
yo no puedo ofenderte, dios, el que tú seas;
ni tú podrías ser ente de ofensa.

Si yo te puedo, y yo lo sé que yo te puedo, oír
todo el misterio que tú eres,
y tú no me lo dices como te lo pregunto,
yo no estoy ofendiéndote.

Y yo sé que te pienso
de la mejor manera que yo quiero,
en verdad de belleza,
belleza de verdad que es mi carrera.
Y, si te pienso así,
yo no puedo ofenderte.

Gracias, yo te las doy siempre. ¿A quién las doy?
A la belleza inmensa, se las doy,
que yo soy bien capaz de conseguir;
que tú has tocado, que eres tú.

Si la belleza inmensa me responde o no,
yo sé que no te ofendo ni la ofendo.

IF IMMENSE BEAUTY ANSWERS ME OR NOT

Searching for you as I am searching,
I cannot offend you, god, whoever you are;
nor are you capable of being offended.

If I am able, and I know I am able to listen
to the whole mystery that you are,
but you refuse to tell me as I ask,
I am not offending you.

And I know I think of you
in the best way I want to,
in the truth of beauty,
beauty of truth that is my career.
And if I think of you so,
I cannot offend you.

I thank you always. To whom am I grateful?
I thank you immense beauty, I am grateful to you,
for I am well able to achieve you;
the one you have touched, the one you are.

If immense beauty answers me or not,
I know I am not offending you, nor do I offend her.

NOTAS

Estos poemas son una anticipación de mi libro *Dios deseante y deseado,* lo último que he escrito en verso, posterior a *Lírica de una Atlántida, Hacia otra desnudez* y *Los olmos de Riverdale.*

Para mí la poesía ha estado siempre íntimamente fundida con toda mi existencia y no ha sido poesía objetiva casi nunca. ¿Y cómo no había de estarlo en lo místico panteísta la forma suprema de lo bello para mí? No que yo haga poesía relijiosa usual; al revés, lo poético lo considero como profundamente relijioso, esa relijión inmanente sin credo absoluto que yo siempre he profesado. Es curioso que, al dividir yo ahora toda mi escritura de verso y prosa en seis volúmenes cronolójicos, por tiempos o épocas mías, y que publicaré con el título jeneral de *Destino,* el final de cada época o tiempo, el final de cada volumen sea de poemas con sentido relijioso.

Es decir, que la evolución, la sucesión, el devenir de lo poético mío ha sido y es una sucesión de encuentro con una idea de dios. Al final de mi primera época, hacia mis veintiocho años, dios se me apareció como en mutua entrega sensitiva; al final de la segunda, cuando yo tenía unos cuarenta años, pasó dios por mí como un fenómeno intelectual, con acento de conquista mutua; ahora, que entro en lo penúltimo de mi destinada época tercera, que supone las otras dos, se me ha atesorado dios como un hallazgo, como una realidad de lo ver-

126

NOTES BY JUAN RAMÓN JIMÉNEZ

These poems are an advance anticipation of my book *God Desiring and Desired*, the last I have written in verse, following *Lírica de Una Atlántida*, *Hacia Otra Desnudez* and *Los Olmos de Riverdale*.

Poetry, for me, has always been intimately fused with the whole of my existence and it has almost never been objective poetry. And why would I not find in mystical pantheism the supreme form of beauty for me? I do not mean to say I am doing religious poetry as commonly understood; just the contrary, poetry I consider to be deeply religious, that immanent religion without absolute dogma which I have always professed. It is a curious fact that now that I am dividing all my writing in verse and prose into six chronological volumes according to times and periods of my own, and which I will publish under the general title of *Destino*, at the end of each period or epoch, and at the end of each volume, I always end with poems that have a religious meaning.

That is to say, the evolution, the succession, the development of my poetry has been and is the development of an encounter with an idea about god. At the end of my first period, when I was about twenty-eight years old, god appeared to me as a mutual sensitive surrender; towards the end of the second, when I was about forty years old, god passed through me as an intellectual phenomenon, with an accent on mutual conquest; now, when I am entering the penultimate stage of my appointed third period, which includes the other two, god has treasured himself within me as a finding, as a reality of what is exact and sufficiently true. If during the first period it was an ecstasy

dadero suficiente y justo. Si en la primera época fue éstasis de amor, y en la segunda avidez de eternidad, en esta tercera es necesidad de conciencia interior y ambiente en lo limitado de nuestro moderado nombre. Hoy concreto yo lo divino como una conciencia única, justa, universal de la belleza que está dentro de nosotros y fuera también y al mismo tiempo. Porque nos une, nos unifica a todos, la conciencia del hombre cultivado único sería una forma de deísmo bastante. Y esta conciencia tercera integra el amor contemplativo y el heroísmo eterno y los supera en totalidad.

Los poemas místicos finales de mi primera y mi segunda época están publicados, en síntesis, en mis libros particulares y en mi *Segunda Antolojía poética*. Y estoy tan lejos ahora de ellos como de mis presentes vitales de esos tiempos, aunque los acepto como recuerdos de días que de cualquier manera son de mi vida.

La escritura poética relijiosa (como la política, la militar, la agrícola, etc.) está para mí en el encuentro después del hallazgo. No se puede escribir esa poesía llamada comunista, por ejemplo, de la que tanto se escribe hoy, sin haber vivido mucho el comunismo, ni desde fuera de un país communista. Una poesía de programa y propaganda de algo que aún no se ha asimilado, por estraordinaria que sea, me parecerá siempre falsa.

Estos poemas los escribí yo mientras pensaba, ya en estas penúltimas de mi vida, repito, en lo que había yo hecho en este mundo para encontrar un dios posible por la poesía. Y pensé entonces que el camino hacia un dios era el mismo que cualquier camino vocativo, el mío de escritor poético, en este caso; que todó mi avance poético en la poesía era avance hacia dios, porque estaba creando un mundo del cual había de ser el fin un dios. Y comprendí que el fin de mi vocación y de mi vida era esta aludida conciencia mejor bella, es decir, jeneral, puesto que para mí todo es o puede ser belleza y poesía, espresión de la belleza.

Mis tres normas vocativas de toda mi vida: la mujer, la obra, la muerte, se me resolvían en conciencia, en comprensión del «hasta qué» punto divino podía llegar lo humano de la gracia del hombre; qué era lo divino que podía venir por el cultivo; cómo el hombre puede ser hombre último con los dones que hemos supuesto a la divinidad encarnada, es decir, enformada.

Hoy pienso que yo no he trabajado en vano en dios, que he trabajado en dios cuanto he trabajado en poesía. Y yo sé que las dos jeneraciones que están ahora tras de mí, están encuadradas en la limitación del realismo mayor; pero también sé que otras jeneraciones más jóvenes han tomado el camino abandonado en nombre de tales virtuosismos asfixiantes; el camino que siguió mi jeneración y que venía ya de la anterior a la mía, camino mucho más real en

of love, and in the second an intense desire for eternity, in this third one it is rather the need for inner consciousness and the limited horizon of our moderate name. Today I define the divine as a unique consciousness, an exact consciousness, a universal consciousness of beauty which is inside ourselves and also outside simultaneously. This is because it unifies, unites us all; this consciousness of the unique, cultivated man would be a form of sufficient deism. This consciousness of my third period integrates contemplative love and eternal heroism and goes beyond them in its totality.

The mystic poems of the end of my first and second periods have been published in synthesis in individual volumes and in my *Segunda Antolojía Poética*. And I am now as distant from them as my vital present is from those times, though I accept them as memories of days which in whatever form, belong to my life.

The religious poetic writing (like the political, military, agricultural, etc.,) is for me an encounter after the finding. It is not possible to write that poetry called Communist, as an example, which is so popular today, not having lived Communism intensely, not from the outside of a Communist country. A poetry of program and propaganda of anything which has not yet become assimilated, regardless of how extraordinary its sound, always sounds false to me.

I wrote these poems while thinking, in these penultimate steps of my life, I repeat, about what I had done in this world to find a god possible through poetry. I then concluded that the way to god was the same as the way of any vocation, mine, as a poetic writer, in this case; all my poetic progress in poetry was a progress towards god, for I was creating a world which had to have as an end a god. Then I understood that the end of my vocation and of my life was the already mentioned better consciousness of beauty, namely the general consciousness of beauty, since for me everything is or can be beauty and poetry and the expression of beauty.

These are the three vocative norms of my life: woman, work, death, and they move about in consciousness, in an effort at understanding up to which divine region the human is able to reach by the grace of what is human; what of the divine can come down through human cultivation; how man can become the ultimate man through the gifts we have transplanted to the incarnate divinity, namely, made flesh.

Today I think I have not labored on god in vain, that I have worked on god to the degree that I have worked on poetry and I know that the two generations that now come after me are framed within the limitations of the greatest realism; but I also know that other younger generations have taken up the abandoned path in the name of such asphyxiating virtuosity; the path my generation followed and which already came from the previous one, a path which is more real in the truest sense, royal path of everything real.

129

el sentido más verdadero, camino real de todo lo real. Con la diferencia que esta es la realidad que está integrada en lo espiritual, como un hueso semillero en la carne de un fruto, y que no escluye un dios vivido por el hombre en forma de conciencia inmanente resuelta en su limitación destinada; conciencia de uno mismo, de su órbita y de su ámbito.

(ANIMAL DE FONDO)

With the difference that this is the reality that is grafted into the spiritual, like a seeding bone in the flesh of its fruit and which does not exclude a god lived by man in the form of an immanent consciousness resolved in its own appointed limitation; consciousness of one self, one's own orbit, and one's own circumstance.

(ANIMAL OF DEPTH)

CAMINO DE FE

(PRÓLOGO INÉDITO DE J. R. J. A *Dios Deseado y Deseante*)

A ti, mi Dios deseado y deseante, solo puedo llegar por fe, fe de niño o fe de viejo.

En mi niñez, niño de España, yo supe de Jesús, el niño Jesús, el niñodiós, como me dijeron y yo decía entonces; y en Jesús, que iba creciendo conmigo, yo fui viendo a mi Dios de entonces, su Padre, el Padrediós, el Padre eterno.

Ya hombre yo empecé a leer lo que dejó dicho, no escrito, Jesús el Nazareno, Jesús el de María, y su palabra clara, sencilla, limpia, jenerosa, buena en suma, me hizo amarlo, esta es la palabra, y tuve fe en su palabra que habló también del Paraíso; y ese Paraíso, el Paraíso de Jesús de Nazaret, lo concebí yo hermoso, hermosísmo. Cuando leí por primera vez lo que Jesús crucificado le dijo al buen ladrón «Esta tarde estarás conmigo en el Paraíso», yo estuve con ellos, y por primera vez, en el Paraíso.

Pero su Padre, el Padre de Jesús el Cristo, de Jesús Poeta y Maestro mío de poesía, del «Maestro Justo» (de que habló Josefo), ¿cómo era para él, cómo es para mí? Pues su palabra era poética, es decir encantadora y misteriosa, hermosísima, era la poesía, la hermosura. Para mí la belleza de la hermosura fue siempre y es más que la llamada verdad, porque es la hermosura de la verdad y de la belleza. Es posible también que la verdad sea más que la belleza porque sea la verdad de la belleza y la hermosura, según se parta de una o de otra. Pero a mí, por Jesús el de la palabra, me lleva la belleza de la hermosura a ser verdadero, independientemente de mi conciencia, es decir, a ser verdadero por naturaleza.

PATH OF FAITH

(Prologue by Juan Ramón Jiménez to *God Desiring and Desired*)

I can only arrive to you, my god desiring and desired, through faith, the faith of a child or that of an old man.

As a child, a child of Spain, I learned of Jesus, the child Jesus, the child-god, as they used to tell me and I used to say; and in Jesus, who kept growing up with me, I began to see the God of then, his Father, the Godfather, the eternal Father.

As a man I started reading what he left behind as said, not written, Jesus the Nazareen, Jesus of Mary, and his clear word, simple, clean, generous, in sum good, made me love him; this was the word, and I had faith in his word too when he spoke of Paradise; and this Paradise, the Paradise of Jesus of Nazareth, I imagined beautiful, very beautiful. When, for the first time, I read what the crucified Jesus said to the good thief: "This afternoon you will be with me in Paradise", I was with them, for the first time in Paradise.

But his Father, the Father of Jesus the Christ, of the Poet Jesus, of my Master in Poetry, of the "Just Master" (of whom Josephus spoke), how was He to him, to me? His word was poetic, that is to say enchanting and mysterious, most beautiful, poetry itself, beauty. The beauty of beauty has always been and is always more than the so called truth, for it is the beauty of truth and of beauty. It is also possible that truth be more than beauty for it might be the truth of beauty and of the beautiful, depending if one starts from one or the other. But for me, the Jesus of the word took me to the beauty of the beautiful to make it true, independently of my consciousness, that is to say, led me to become true by nature.

Contemplando la belleza, yo no puedo ser lo que se dice malo, que yo no sé lo que pueda ser cuando se ama puesto que concibo lo malo como odio; y por la belleza yo me uno con la vida toda, más que con la llamada verdad. Quiero decir que yo estoy más seguro de lo que es belleza que de lo que es verdad, según las normas. Y cuando digo belleza no digo estética, como algunos críticos míos han creído más o menos justamente, no digo belleza científica ni artística, ni como ejemplo, sino como naturaleza, como esa inmensa naturaleza tan artificial naturalmente en la que no hay nada malo, nada odioso, sino destino inmenso. La ciencia y el arte son nada más que el vaso suficiente en que doy la belleza y que pretendo que sean lo que deben ser, que sean cuidados como serían mis manos si yo diese en ellas como vaso a los demás mi propia sangre. Pero el vaso se queda en la mano y la ambrosía se bebe y llega a los tuétanos. Esa ambrosía embriagadora es la belleza inmensamente espresada pues que la belleza es inmensa; el vaso, el poema cantado o escrito o hablado debe ser inmensamente sencillo y trasparente, pero de todos modos es vaso, es cuerpo, es mano y yo puedo beber en mi mano agua informe a menos que un equilibrio milagroso me haga sostener en mi mano el chorro de la fuente tal como sale. Pero entonces ya no hay vaso, y ese milagro solo lo puede dar el canto enloquecido, y no es posible estar locos siempre; mejor, hay que olvidarse de que somos locos permanentes o cuerdos permanentes. En ese punto del olvido estaría la espresión poética.

Yo sé que si Jesús está en el Paraíso que prometió al ladrón, con su Padre, allí llegaré yo con los que amo, que yo creo en la palabra del Cristo como creyó el ladrón, por su belleza, pues sin duda el buen ladrón era un poeta; y allí estará el Padre que Jesús no me dijo cómo era, como es, y yo no me lo puedo figurar. Jesús vio la belleza en su verdad y yo veo mi verdad en la belleza, en la belleza natural y en la belleza moral, ideal, espiritual de ese espíritu ideal y moral que Jesús encomendó desde la cruz a su Padre; la belleza que él dijo a todos que era el amor, su fe primera.

Esa es mi fe, Jesús de mi vejez, la fe de mi vejez en ti que me fuiste viejo, el amor a todo lo que veo, a todo lo que siente. Esa es mi fe porque la veo, ver la belleza en todo lo que miro o mejor mirar bello todo lo que veo. Y yo sé que por Jesús de Marta y de María, otra María que no era su madre, que el Padre es el amor original, que eso quiere decir Dios, manantial, y en ese amor por fe Jesús y yo nos hallaremos en Dios un día con los nuestros porque los nuestros serán nosotros en este amanecer en que lo pienso, este mismo día, hoy que abre sobre toda la naturaleza que me rodea, tan hermoso como el hoy sin fin de aquel Paraíso que el Cristo ofreció al que tuvo fe.

Hermosura, belleza, Paraíso, este es el Paraíso, sí, y en él estoy desde que nací, desde que desperté de otra clase de sueño, y en él vivo. Y si en él vive siempre mi conciencia, mi conciencia del Paraíso, sobreviviré en él, en él,

Contemplating beauty I cannot be what is called bad, for I do not know what one may become when one loves, since I conceive evil as hate; and through beauty I joined the whole of life, more so than with the so called truth. I mean by this that I am more sure of what is beautiful than I am of what is true, according to the norms. And when I say beauty I do not mean aesthetics, as some of my critics have said with more or less exactness, I do not mean scientific or artistic beauty either, not even as an example, but as a nature, the immense artificial nature where there is nothing evil, nothing hateful, but only an immense project. Science and art are no more than the sufficient glass where I serve beauty and which I pretend are what they ought to be, that they be taken care of the way I take care of my hands if with them, as in a glass, I served my own blood to other to drink. The glass remains in the hands and the scent is drunk and reaches our marrow. This inebriating scent is beauty immensely expressed, for beauty is immense; the glass, the sung, written or spoken poem must be immensely simple and transparent; but it always remains a glass, a body, a hand so that I may be able to drink in my hand shapeless water, unless a miraculous equilibrium might allow me to hold in my hand the gush of water as it comes pouring out of the fountain. But then there would be no glass, and the miracle could only be produced when the song goes totally mad, and there is no way to be always derranged; it is better to forget that we are permanently crazy people or that we are permanently normal people. On this point of forget-fulness the poetic expression stands.

I know that if Jesus is in the Paradise that he promised the good thief, with his Father, then there I will go with those I love, for, because of its beauty, I believe in the word of Christ as the thief did, for the good thief, no doubt, was a poet; and there I will find the Father that I am free to imag-ine, for Jesus never told me how He was, how He is. Jesus saw beauty in his truth and I see my truth in beauty, in natural and moral beauty, ideal, spir-itual form of an ideal and moral spirit which Jesus commended to his Father from the Cross; the beauty he proclaimed to all to be love, his first faith.

That is my faith, Jesus of my old age, the faith of my old age in you who became old with me, the love for everything I see, for all that feels. This is my faith because I see it. I see beauty in all I look at or, even better, I see the beautiful in all I see. And I know that Jesus of Martha and Mary, the other Mary who was not his mother, that the Father is the original love, for this is what God means, the spring, and through that love in faith, Jesus and I will meet in God one day with our own. For our own will be ourselves on this morning I am thinking of, this day itself, the day that he opens over all of nature surrounding me, a day as beautiful as the day without end of that Paradise that Christ offered to the one who had faith.

Beauty, beauty, Paradise, this is Paradise, yes and in it I am since my birth, since I woke up from another kind of dream and in the raw. And if in it my consciousness is always alive, my consciousness of Paradise, I will live

aquí donde están el Cristo y el Padre si los sabemos comprender por su palabra dicha y nuestra palabra espresada. Yo puedo ir a la palabra que es Jesús para mí por mi camino propio, por mi palabra y por ella voy. Voy a su palabra sin adorno, sin vano comentario escolástico, sin santos padres, sin Papas, sin muros, voy a su palabra aislada de El Libro como a un campo de margaritas en primavera humana o como un espejo de luz en el humano invierno.

La muerte será solo entonces el descanso eterno y grato del día eterno que así será sueño eterno de hermoso ensueño.

in it, in it, where Christ and the Father are if we are able to understand them through the word said and our expressed word. I can go to the word that is Jesus by my own path, through my word and with it I go. I am going to this word with no ornaments, with no useless scholastic commentary, with no Holy Fathers, no Popes, no walls; I am going to his word isolated from the Book as to a field of daisies in the human spring, or as to a mirror of light in the human winter.

Death will then only be the eternal and grateful rest of the eternal day which thus will become the eternal dream of beautiful dreaming.